Moonville Whispers
Unearthing Ghosts Along the Haunted Hocking Hills Rail Trail

ISBN- 978-1-940087-74-0

Written and illustrated by Jannette Quackenbush

 Jannette Quackenbush is an author of over 50 books, folklorist, naturalist, and paranormal researcher. She focuses on ghost stories, folklore, and hiking trails in the Appalachian and southern U.S. Known for her engaging storytelling, she has published many works on local legends and haunted places. Her project, "Dark Journeys with Jannette," features guided hikes where participants explore haunted sites and learn about the region's folklore, connecting them to the rich cultural history and stories of the area. People always ask me, "Do you believe?" And here is how I feel, "Everybody is a skeptic until they experience something out of the norm. Then, all of a sudden, they realize there is more out there to discover, and they become part of this big community of others whose eyes are open to the unknown. And they want to know more, see more, adventure more. Do I believe? Well, I'd certainly rather be racing out to be with the believers, the adventurous ones who get out and explore. You can be among this community too—just get out there!"

The Marietta & Cincinnati Railroad was built to connect Ohio's eastern river port at Marietta with western markets in Cincinnati, opening the coal, iron, clay, and timber-rich hills of southern and central Ohio to trade and settlement. Its route through the remote section of southeastern Ohio was chosen specifically to tap those natural resources and link isolated mining and industrial towns to the state's growing rail network. Moonville would be among them.

*Local folklore claims that Samuel Coe wrote a letter convincing the railroad to run its line through Moonville, but historical evidence doesn't support that story. The route was chosen by surveyors following the Raccoon Creek valley to reach **clay, coal, iron, and timber resources**—including the **fine clays that supplied the region's large pottery, ceramics, and brick industry**, which thrived in nearby towns such as **McArthur, Creola, Nelsonville, and Crooksville**, as well as the **iron ore and hardwood needed to fire the great furnaces of the Hanging Rock Iron Region**. These were practical needs, driven by the expanding demand for industrial materials and the goal of connecting Ohio's interior to national trade routes—not personal influence.*

Along the Marietta and Cincinnati Railroad:

The Ghost Towns

Route: Zaleski → Hope Furnace → Hope Furnace Station → Moonville → King's Station → Ingham Station → Mineral City (Waterloo)

Zaleski → Hope Furnace Station: 3.2 miles

Hope Furnace Station → Moonville 1.7 miles

Moonville → Ingham Station 1.5 miles

Ingham Station → King's Station 0.7 miles

King's Station → Mineral 1.4 miles

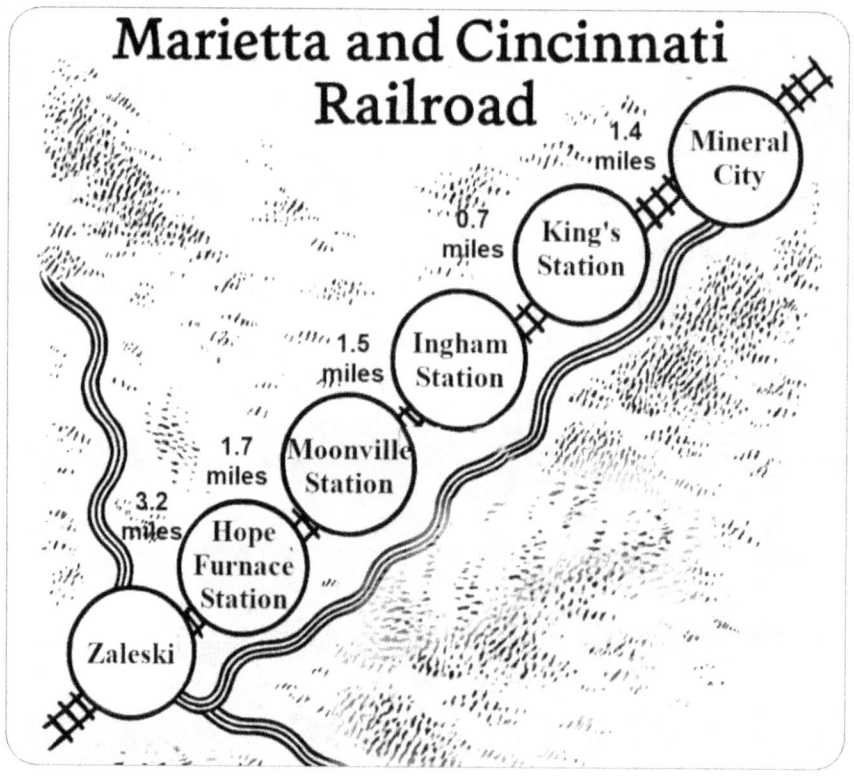

When the Marietta & Cincinnati Railroad carved through the hills of Vinton and Athens counties in the mid-1800s, it stitched together a line of soon-to-be towns—born for coal, timber, and iron and destined to die just as fast. The train didn't just carry passengers and freight. It carried whole communities. Along its tracks, towns were planted like seeds—and most just as quickly withered. Zaleski. Hope Furnace. Hope Furnace Station. Moonville. King's Station. Ingham. Mineral/Waterloo. Some thrived only briefly. Others, like Zaleski and Mineral, still hold scattered homes and quiet remnants of life. But most faded beneath the weight of exhaustion, busted seams, and time. And yet, the dead didn't leave.

Zaleski
(GPS along Trail: 39.286275, -82.390131)
Distance to Hope Furnace Station: 3.2 miles

The village of Zaleski was one of the first communities shaped by the coming of the railroad. Originally a hub for timber and later iron and coal, it fed the early industry of the region. It served as a branching point for the Hope Furnace spur. Zaleski remains inhabited today, but many of its rail-era neighbors have vanished into the woods.

Hope Furnace
(GPS *off-trail*: 39.332062, -82.340525)

Hope Furnace was first among the ghost towns. The massive charcoal iron furnace was fired up in the 1850s and built near Big Sandy Run as part of Ohio's booming iron industry. A small community supported the furnace with housing for workers, a general store, and access to the railroad.

The foundation of the old furnace still stands, tall and crumbling. Some say on certain nights, you can see flickers of a lantern near the stack.

Hope Furnace Station
(GPS along trail: 39.318199, -82.343751)
Distance to Moonville: 1.7 miles

A short distance beyond the furnace itself, Hope Furnace Station became a hub of coal mining and railroad traffic. Unlike the iron-focused furnace site, this station supported nearby coal shafts. It served as a crucial stop for loading ore and passengers. It developed into a separate identity, with its own mining camp and spur track connecting back to the Marietta & Cincinnati line. The station eventually declined with the mines, but the ghost of its activity lingers—workers trudging in silence, phantom whistles blowing in the dark.

Moonville
(GPS along trail: 39.308438, -82.324532)
Distance to Ingham Station: 1.5 mile

A few miles up the line, Moonville appeared—barely a town at all, just a cluster of houses built by the Coe and Ferguson families who sold land to the railroad. There was a sawmill, a boarding house/grocery, a couple of mining outposts—and the notorious Moonville Tunnel.

The town was isolated. Residents walked the tracks to reach anything beyond. Many died on them. Between the narrow tunnel, many trestles, and steep cuts in the hills, there was nowhere to run from an oncoming train. Even today, people whisper about figures on the tracks and a ghost with a lantern near the tunnel entrance.

Ingham Station
(GPS along trail: 39.311799, -82.300095)

Distance to King's Station: 0.7 miles

Just a mile and a half past Moonville stood Ingham Station, a larger outpost. It briefly had a post office in the early 1900s, supporting nearby miners and railway workers. Old roadbeds still lead into the woods from the track, where homes and shafts once stood. Now, it is forest and silence—except when it is not. Hikers have reported strange lights, spectral footsteps, and an overwhelming sense of being watched along the trail between Moonville and Ingham.

King's Station (King Hollow)
(GPS along trail: 39.317229, -82.288802)

Distance to Mineral/Waterloo: 1.4 miles

Further west lay King's Station, founded by Silas King. He saw the train as an opportunity and opened mines on his land, building a town around them—complete with a saloon, store, schoolhouse, and post office. His son, "Doc" King, kept it alive a little longer, running a store and watering hole from his own home. The tracks here pass through the crooked wooden ribs of King Tunnel, a timber-lined passage still standing today. But the mines dried out, the post office closed in 1894, and King's Station collapsed. Now, only the tunnel remains—along with rumors of something still crawling through it.

Waterloo / Mineral City
(GPS along trail: 39.324774, -82.265220)

A mile farther, the rail reached Mineral City—a mining town established directly by the rail company.

It had businesses, stores, a doctor, and housing for miners and their families. It thrived in the 1880s, supported by coal.

But like the others, it was a town with an expiration date. When the coal ran out, so did most of the businesses. But some residents have tarried, their homes still a cozy sight when passing through this remote community.

The oldest buildings crumbled. Some vanished under brush and vines. But at night, people say you can still hear the faint cry of a train that no longer runs... and sometimes, something following in its wake.

A Line of Ghosts

From Zaleski to Hope Furnace, and on to Mineral/Waterloo, the Marietta & Cincinnati Railroad (later the Baltimore and Ohio Railroad) bound these lost towns together as it head toward Luhrig and Athens. When the train stopped, the trees took over.

The iron rails were torn up and taken away.

The wooden ties were tossed by the wayside.

Houses fell in. But not everything left.

Today, the Moonville Rail Trail follows the path of that line. The ghosts of these towns—miners, children, cats, broken men, forgotten women—still walk the gravel, cross the trestles, and pass through the tunnels.

Not gone. Not resting. Just quieter now. Until someone comes close enough to hear them.

The Place Called Moonville

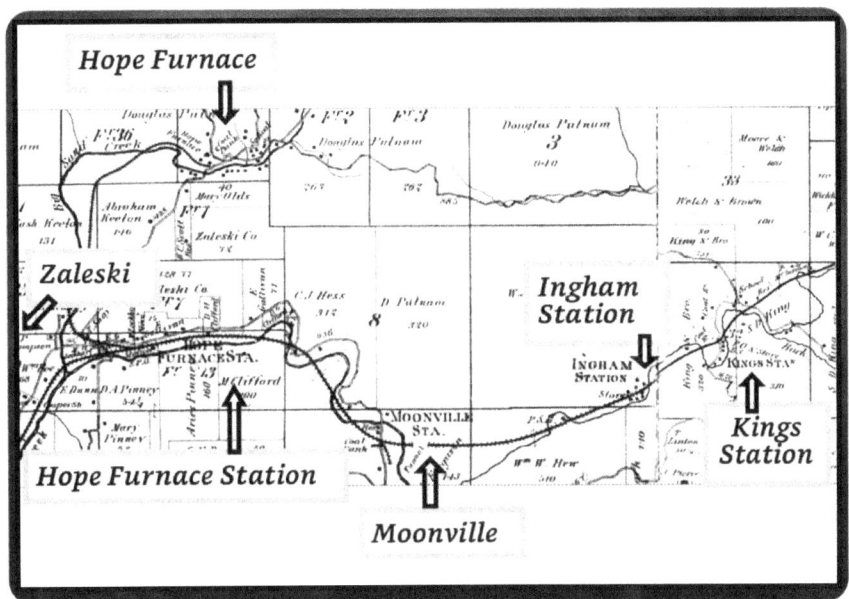

When most imagine Moonville, they picture a bustling town—streets lined with homes and storefronts, smoke curling from chimneys, neighbors calling to one another from porches.

But the truth is, Moonville was never much of a town at all. Just a handful of family homes stood there, tucked into a deep fold of southeastern Ohio's Vinton County along Raccoon Creek.

It began with two families: Henry and Rhoda Ferguson, who worked the land, and Samuel and Emeline Coe, who ran a coal mine and operated a sawmill far from any main road.

These families lived quiet, isolated lives in a stretch of wilderness where the trees pressed close, and the hills were steep and unforgiving.

Part of a Bigger Picture

But to talk about Moonville, you have to look beyond the tiny patch of clearing where those early families lived. It was part of something larger—an emerging network of industry and survival. In those days, Zaleski and Big Sand Furnace (what would later be called Hope Furnace) were the only nearby settlements of real size, both driven by iron production.

But they were hard to reach. There were no proper roads—just crude dirt paths and creek beds that flooded in spring and froze solid in winter.

To move goods and coal to the furnaces, and to have any hope of connecting with the outside world, the Fergusons and Coes petitioned Vinton County commissioners to extend the narrow road that followed Raccoon Creek from Bolin Mills (along the old route from Chillicothe through McArthur to Athens).

The request was granted.

The road was built, climbing the sandstone hills and weaving past the creek beds until it linked the Coe and Ferguson properties to Zaleski and Hope Furnace.

Even so, travel remained slow. The region needed more.

The Iron Line Through the Trees

Around that same time, the Marietta & Cincinnati Railroad pushed eastward, hunting coal seams and freight lines through the region's remote hills.

Their surveyors mapped a route that cut directly between the Ferguson and Coe properties.

The company built trestles over the winding waterways and blasted a tunnel through the high ridge behind the Ferguson homestead. They laid down track and built a small station on the Coe property.

The area was named Moonville—not for any person, but for the way the full moon seemed to rest over the tunnel mouth at certain times of year, watching from above like a pale, silent witness.

With the railroad in place, other coal mining towns soon followed: Ingham Station, King's Station, Mineral, and Luhrig. None of these places existed before the trains came through. Moonville sat at the center of it all—a fixed point on the iron artery that kept the region alive. People passed through it constantly, traveling between the mining towns, sawmills, and iron furnaces. The trains were used for hauling coal and those who managed to hitch a ride. With no roads cut through the dense Rew Forest stretching for miles on either side, the railway became the only reliable path. Folks walked the tracks because there was nowhere else to walk.

The Tracks That Took Their Toll

The rail line ran straighter than the roads and higher than the floodplain. It became a path of sorts—a foot trail worn down by laborers and families alike.

Men walked it to reach the mines. Women took it to fetch supplies from nearby towns. Children crossed it to reach scattered schools. But there was only one set of tracks.

Eastbound and westbound trains shared the same line.

Accidents were frequent. People were struck, dragged, and thrown into the creeks.

Sometimes, they never made it home.

Over the years, too many died along that line—so many that folks stopped calling it bad luck and started calling it something else. A place like Moonville, where people passed through but didn't always make it out, doesn't stay quiet forever.

The stories started as whispers—low and uneasy. They rode the wind through the trees and curled along the rails. People who walked past the old wreck sites began to feel watched. Some heard footsteps behind them. Others saw figures standing too still near the trestles. They spoke of men torn apart by steel and speed, of women struck down in the dark, and of how the dead didn't seem to stay buried. Some said they came back. Others said they never left.

When the mines went dry and the work ran out, the towns around Moonville began to rot where they stood. Houses buckled. Doors hung open to the wind. The noise of industry faded, and the woods crept back in. The last freight train passed through in 1985. By 1988, the tracks were torn up and carried away—over thirty miles gone.

But the dead?

The dead stayed.

And that's where the stories begin.

The Bigger Picture

Before stepping deeper into Moonville, it's crucial to understand the surrounding communities that formed its Bigger Picture—for it was from these neighboring towns that travelers set out, following paths destined to cross Moonville.

Each place had its own share of hauntings, ghostly encounters interwoven with Moonville's own lingering spirits—often linked by family ties, friendships, and lives shared across these communities.

Zaleski

Hope Furnace

Hope Furnace Station

Moonville

Ingham Station

King's Station

Mineral

McArthur

The Town: Zaleski

Zaleski in its early days

Zaleski was meant to be a model mining town—plotted and laid out in 1856 at the edge of the wilderness, where the coal ran deep and the woods pressed in close.

It was named for Count Peter F. Zaleski, a Polish-born financier and mining official who helped back the Marietta & Cincinnati Railroad and its expansion into Vinton County. The town bore his name.

At its height, Zaleski boasted a roaring blast furnace, seven general stores, several churches, brickyards, a flour mill, two doctors, a Masonic lodge, a schoolhouse, and fifteen saloons packed shoulder-to-shoulder with miners and iron men.

Smoke curled from chimneys day and night. Coal carts clattered through the streets. Over 1,500 people lived there at its peak, most of them tied in one way or another to the furnace or the railway.

In 1859, Francis Hazeltine took over the management of the furnace and built a home called 'Zaleski Castle' on a hill overlooking the town. It became a venue for social gatherings but later fell into ruins.

For a time, Zaleski thrived. The railroad cut straight through its heart, hauling out iron and bringing in workers, goods, and news from beyond. Like many towns built on coal and ore, Zaleski burned hot—bright with industry, loud with promise—and then burned low.

Zaleski Today

The fires never fully went out, but the light dimmed.

And the world moved on.

What was once a boomtown slipped quietly toward obscurity.

And as the rails stretched deeper into the woods, other towns rose in their wake—each with their own whispered warnings and shadowed tales.

But it was in Zaleski, perhaps, that the first of these ghostly echoes began.

Zaleski Ghost Story: White Thing of Powder Plant Road

Powder Plant Road, named for the explosives factory along its path, slips quietly from Zaleski into open farmland and dense woods. About a mile and a half out, just past the low bridge over Raccoon Creek, the paved road makes a sharp, sudden bend. Most travelers turn left here toward familiar lights.

But a few keep straight—a shorter, lonelier route once called Infirmary Road.

Infirmary Road cuts rough through the countryside. Gravel scatters beneath wheels and hooves, echoing sharp and hollow. Farms lie scattered along its length, separated by tangled brush and patches of dense woodland. Thick limbs arch overhead, blotting out the moon and swallowing travelers whole. Leaves rot thick beneath the canopy, air heavy with mold and damp earth.

At night, silence settles fast here, broken only by faint rustles of unseen things creeping in the brush.

People avoided this road after dark.

They knew what lived there.

Something White in the Dark

In the late 1800s, Alonzo Eckelberry—a sober, steady farmer known by everyone in Zaleski—rode along Infirmary Road, eager for home. The sun had already dropped below the hills, shadows gathering swiftly. Just past Herrold's Mill along the banks of Raccoon Creek, his horse shied suddenly, hooves scraping nervously on gravel.

Something moved beside him.

Eckelberry turned sharply. At first, he saw only darkness and brush, tangled branches shivering faintly. Then, from the gloom, a pale shape slipped forward.

Silent.

Featureless.

It moved smoothly, matching the pace of his horse, gliding like smoke just beyond his stirrup.

He kicked his horse into a faster trot.

The thing kept pace.

When he slowed again, breath caught tight in his throat, the shape slowed with him, ghostly white and silent as frost.

He leaned forward, urging his horse into a gallop, pulse hammering hard in his ears.

It wouldn't let go.

The Ride Behind

As Eckelberry approached a small, isolated farmhouse, the pale thing moved suddenly—lunging from roadside shadows onto the horse's back.

It hopped on the horse with him!

Coldness spilled across him, raw and bitter. He jerked around sharply, dread squeezing tight in his chest.

It had no eyes. No face.

Just white emptiness.

Eckelberry shouted, kicking wildly at his mount's sides, spinning the animal in a frantic circle. He felt the thing's presence pressing nearer, the chill biting through clothing, seeping deep into his bones.

It was holding on.

He whipped the reins toward Zaleski, racing back the way he had come. Behind him, the thing stayed perched silently, motionless but there, real as the animal beneath him. Only at Shry Hill did he feel the sudden, sickening lift as it left him, sliding silently back into roadside brush. Eckelberry didn't slow until town lights warmed his face, voices calling his name.

He never rode that road after dusk again.

The White Thing is Still There

These days, cars whip past that lonely stretch of road without a second glance, the drivers unaware of what watches from the woods—what waits, still and patient, for someone to pass.

Some say the ghost appears in the backseat when you drive through that shadowed bend. A silent hitchhiker looking for a ride—or something else.

You don't see it at first.

But it's there.

A pale figure.

White. Still.

No eyes.

No face.

Just the shape of it, sitting quietly in the rearview mirror.

Not moving.

Not blinking.

Then when *you* blink. It vanishes.

Or so you hope.

But when you finally gather the nerve to turn around—to really look—it's STILL THERE.

Zaleski Ghost Story: The Thing in the Hollow that Watches at Zaleski Iron Furnace

Just beyond the last houses of Zaleski, where the woods grow close, and the hills begin to rise, there were once Adena burial mounds—broad, ancient forms—and a great earthen fortress built by a people who knew how to shape the land without breaking it.

They stood for thousands of years.

Then came the settlers. Then came the furnace.

Nearly all the mounds were leveled.

The fortress flattened.

Stone dragged in. Timber stripped.

And the Zaleski Company Iron Furnace rose where the dead had once been honored.

Where the road bends along Mine Hollow, hardly any ruins of the old furnace still stand beneath the Forestry Division lot. The land around it was once thick with coalin' roads—muddy black paths where men cut back the forest and dug deep into the coal seams to keep the stacks alive. Even now, you can see the bony dumps along the roadside—mountains of waste coal abandoned to rot. And only the orange-red acid mine drainage bleeding through the creek beds reveals where the furnace once stood.

It was built hot and fast in the 1850s.

Its fireboxes burned through storms, through injuries, through winters that split stone.

Ore wagons clattered through the forest.

Men shoveled without pause.

No one talked about the sounds that came from the stacks after midnight.

When the fires finally went out, the furnace didn't die.

It grew silent.

It held its breath.

The Hollow That Watches

Years passed. The men moved on. But something stayed behind. People who passed that way said the air felt wrong.

Too still. Too quiet.

They spoke of wind whispering through windowless arches, sounding like hammers on steel.

But no one worked there anymore.

Even now, where only a hollow and one or two broken boulders remain where the furnace stood, the air still shifts when you walk too close.

The wind moves through the trees—but it doesn't sound right.

Sometimes, there's hammering.

One knock. Then silence.

One man swore he heard a voice: "Keep it burning."

But there was no one there.

Some say you feel it before you see it. A sudden pressure on your back, like someone standing too close.

"My granddad said the ruins rang like stone drums at dusk... a knock—then silence."

"When the wind dies down... no birds. No crickets. Just emptiness."

If you ride past on that narrow stretch of Mine Hollow Road, you might glimpse it in the last pocket of woods just before getting to Route 278— a flash of black shadow on the hillside.

A dark, dark silhouette pacing the top of the hillock where the furnace stood, slow, steady, like it's still checking the embers.

Then nothing.

Only trees and rubble and coal-pocked earth.

Only heavy stone and fallen shadow.

What Was Broken

It doesn't speak. It doesn't follow.

But something was stirred when men dug into those hills—pulling coal from the earth like marrow from bone. And worse, when they tore down the mounds, flattened the fortress, and built fire atop sacred ground.

That land was never meant to burn.

Some say the digging woke it.

Others say the burning did.

Whatever watches that hollow now didn't die with the furnace.

 It didn't fade with the men.

 It brought them back—pieces of their souls— and keeps them working.

Working.

Working.

It stayed.

They stayed.

It waits.

They wait.

And when the wind dies, when the trees hold their breath, and that road feels too narrow beneath your feet—

They watch.

They wait.

And maybe—they are waiting for you.

The Town: Hope Furnace

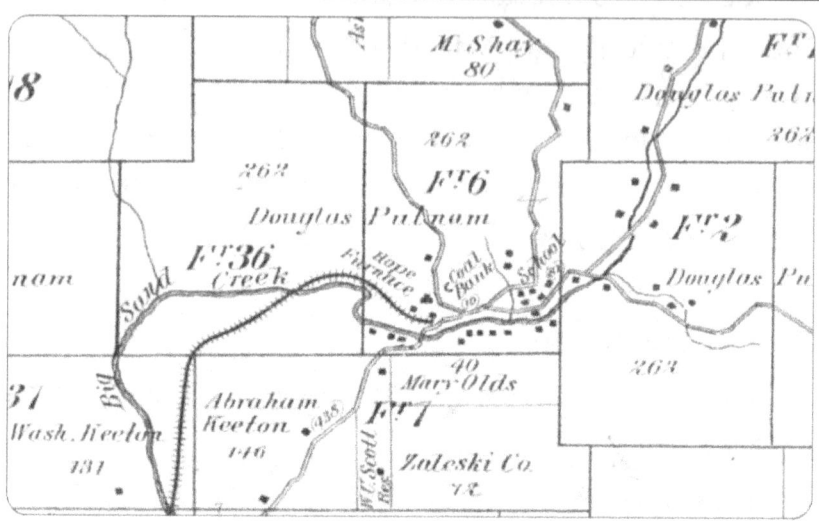

The Hope Furnace would have looked much like the Hecla Furnace pictured.

Once known as Big Sand Furnace, named for the stream it bordered—Big Sandy Run—the place later became Hope Furnace, one of 69 charcoal iron furnaces scattered through Ohio's Hanging Rock Iron Region.

It roared to life in 1854 and burned hard until 1874. For twenty years, its fires never truly went out.

Smelting iron took an army. Hundreds of men worked the surrounding woods and hills—cutting timber, digging ore, burning charcoal in the dark forest, and driving oxen carts heavy with iron. The woods never rested. Smoke rolled through the hollows. Trees fell fast. The hills bled.

From a small rail spur at Hope Furnace Station, a single horse pulled a loaded railcar uphill to the furnace, where teams of soot-blackened men fed it to the flames. The finished iron was hauled back down, the horse trudging the same track again and again.

A town sprang up to support it: a blacksmith shop, storage sheds, wagon works, office buildings. Across the road, rows of worker homes stood shoulder to shoulder. Hope Furnace School sat just over the ridge—once the largest in the district, with nearly a hundred students packed inside.

The ruins of Hope Furnace today.

Now, it's all gone.

The school.

The houses.

The noise.

Only a crumbling stone stack remains, looming above the roadside like a tomb marker. Across the way, where hundreds once lived and died, a silent pine grove sways over moss-covered foundation stones.

The ragged path into the ghost town—Olds Hollow Trail and the area of the old settlement where workers' homes once stood.

There's little left to show they were ever here.

Except for the stories. And the ghosts.

Hope Furnace Ghost Story: The Night Watchman Returns

For twenty years, the furnace burned hot and constant—its appetite fed by the charcoal men, the ox teams, and the timber cutters.

The iron trade thrived. The woods thinned. And then the ghost came.

They say he was a nightshift worker—one of the nameless, soot-faced men who dragged his body through the dark for barely a dollar a day.

The Fall

On the night he died, he had just stepped from the storage shed, arms heavy with tools and grit, a lantern swinging from his hand. He crossed the narrow wooden bridge to the stack—a triangular mass of stone, blackened with years of fire and ore. Somewhere near the top, carts dumped raw charcoal, iron ore, and limestone through a trapdoor into the blaze below.

But that night, the door wasn't shut.

And he never saw the edge.

The floor swallowed him.

The fire took the rest.

They say he didn't scream.

They say the furnace did.

The Lantern Returns

Not long after, when the company men met in the general office to tally profits and cut wages, the silence would shatter with a sudden, thunderous BOOM-BOOM-BOOM on the door.

A fist.

Heavy.

Demanding.

But when they opened it—no one.

Just fog. Just black.

The door shut.

Then again—

BOOM. BOOM. BOOM.

The thudding grew louder. Angrier.

Some said the hinges warped. Others said it was the ironworker, burned down to bone and rage, still trying to be counted.

Later, long after the furnace cooled and the buildings slouched into ruin, the light returned.

A lantern.

Floating.

Dragging itself through the dark.

It followed the dead man's path—rising from the back sheds, crossing the long-gone bridge, moving steadily to the stack. Always to the stack. They say it weaves as if clutched in a ruined hand. As if the body is still walking, though there's nothing left but ash.

The structure is bare now—only the stone shell remains. The bridge is gone. The carts rotted. The path was overtaken by weeds. But the light still comes.

And if you stand down by the grassy bottomland, near the parking lot where the woods press close and the earth still smells scorched—

You might hear it.

That same, low-knuckled thunder.

BOOM.

BOOM.

BOOM.

Not on wood. Not on metal.

On something deeper.

Something that doesn't rot.

Something still alive beneath the ruin.

And it wants out.

Here is how a local told the story—

Mr. Mike Shea

"When Hope Furnace was in operation, one of the workers fell down the stack at night with his lantern into the white hot ore. Later on people claimed that on some nights they'd see him on top of the stack with his lantern. At the big store at the furnace one night, some fellows inside heard a knock on the door and when they opened it no one was there. They thought it was him coming back—this happened several times—"

As told by Mike Shea, Aug 16, 1961 to Bill Price

Hope Furnace Ghost Story: The Burnt Cabin in Olds Hollow

Beneath the Pines

The land that was once bustling with the Hope Iron Furnace town is now covered by a lush pine forest. Birds chirp in the treetops, and squirrels scamper along the forest floor. Hikers follow the narrow, winding trail past trickling waterfalls and small recess caves, unaware of the secrets this dark forest hides beneath a hundred years of dead pine needles.

But something listens beneath the hush.

Something waits.

Not everyone who lived here left.

And not everyone who died stayed down.

The Coaler's Shack

After the war, when the iron furnace still choked smoke into the hills, two brothers worked as coalers—cutting timber, charring it down in pits to feed the stack. It was hard labor, filthy and thankless. Their cabin sat off the main trail, a one-room lean-to cobbled together from scrap and split wood, thin-walled and always cold.

In mid-November, when the nights bit hard, and frost glazed the brush, their cabin caught fire, the hollow lit up with orange glow and smoke that curled like fingers through the trees. By the time neighbors reached it, the shack was gone—nothing left but black timber and the stink of burned flesh.

When they sifted through the wreckage, they found only warped iron, splinters of bone, and a reek so sharp it stung the nose long after you left it behind. The bones were burned through, brittle as leaves, crumbling at the edges when moved.

No autopsy. No investigation. Everyone assumed one of the brothers, maybe both, tried to spark heat using what they had on hand—camphene. It was a poor man's lantern oil, a volatile mix of turpentine, alcohol, and camphor. One careless touch could light a blaze hotter than the furnace itself.

That was the story they settled on.

Two coffins were lowered into the earth.

They blamed the camphene. Called it an accident. Moved on.

Whispers in the Ash

Winter passed, then spring. The hollow quieted again. But those who walked the trail through the woods began to speak of strange things. Low voices echoing through the pines. Shouting, distant and harsh, like two men locked in an argument that never ended. Sometimes, it came at dusk, other times in the deep hours before dawn.

The sounds came from the direction of the ruin. But when anyone looked, there was no one there. No fresh tracks. No sign of life. Just the black, half-buried stones of a forgotten foundation, and the sour reek of something old and chemical that lingered in the air like a warning.

Some said the forest had a memory.

Others said it had a grudge.

The Man Who Watched Them Burn

Five years later, in Tennessee, a man named John Slavens was arrested for killing his own nephew. It was a brutal crime. He didn't deny it. He was tried, convicted, and sentenced. But before he could be taken to prison, his wife came forward and confessed to something darker.

She said it wasn't his first time.

She said he'd murdered two other young men—years ago, in Ohio. They'd just been paid for their work at a furnace, she said. Slavens had followed them, robbed them, and beaten them dead inside their cabin.

He poured camphene across the floor and walls, lit a match, and walked away as the fire took hold.

John Slavens never looked back.

The Rope and the Pines

Word spread fast. Too fast.

A mob gathered before the prison could move him. They stormed the jail, dragged Slavens from his cell, and took him to a tree outside town. No trial. No sermon. They threw a rope over the branch and hanged him until the body sagged and the forest around him went still.

Justice by hand. No one spoke his name again.

But in Olds Hollow, something changed.

What Remains

The cabin is gone now. The forest has swallowed every trace but a few crumbling stones where its foundation once sat. Fallen needles cover the ground like a blanket, thick and matted, untouched by wind.

But those who walk the Olds Hollow Trail—especially near Sandy Run—know something still lingers.

They've heard voices—sharp, panicked, cracking with heat.

They've heard screaming.

Not the echo of it. The fresh kind. The kind that tears from a throat. The kind a man makes when he knows the fire's too fast to outrun.

Some say they've heard footsteps too. Heavy. Measured. Not running—but walking. As if someone still circles the site. It's as if John Slavens still comes back to watch what he's done.

The steps draw near.

Then stop.

Always just behind.

Those who turn to look see nothing.

But the smell of burnt oil lingers.

And the pines don't sway.

Something old is still speaking.

But not to be heard.

To be relived.

Screamed. Walked. Watched.

Over and over again.

And one night, it may not *stop* behind you.

The Town: Hope Furnace Station

The Shea property at Hope Furnace Station. Many homes once dotted this roadway, almost all are gone.

Tucked in the hollows between Zaleski and Moonville, Hope Furnace Station was more than just a waystop. It was a raw-boned mining and rail camp carved out by fire, iron, and the Marietta and Cincinnati Railway. During the peak years of the Zaleski Company's hold on the land, the surrounding hills rang with the sound of axes, blasting powder, and the grinding echo of coal carts.

The old Hope Furnace Station Schoolhouse was moved from its location near State Route 278 to Wheelabout Road. It is often confused as being the Hope Furnace Schoolhouse that was razed by a local county commissioner's private hunting club.

Homes rose in crooked lines above the floodbanks of Raccoon Creek, nestled tight to the tracks where the main line ran like a scar across the earth.

A spur split off there—narrow and rust-riddled— veering straight toward Hope Furnace and its smoking stack.

The families who settled here—Sheas, Pinneys, Keetons, Lockharts, Fees, and Dunns—built their lives close to the heat of the iron furnace, the clatter of the railroad, and the dreams of making it rich on black diamonds—coal.

Hope Furnace Station experienced its share of tragedies, and some left marks that didn't fade. In the late 1800s, a man named Edmund Dunn—a known scoundrel by many accounts—ran a shabby grocery and bar near the tracks, before there were real laws governing who could buy what. He was known for turning a blind eye, especially if coin changed hands.

The old Hope Furnace Station church, Hope Chapel, along Wheelabout Road.

One of his regulars was a 14-year-old boy named Michael Clifford. Edmund Dunn had sold him strong liquor more than once, no questions asked. On the night of January 18, 1877, things turned sour. The two got into an argument—some say over payment.

Others say the boy came back mean, drunk, and wild-eyed. What's certain is that the quarrel ended with Dunn bleeding out on the dusty floor, stabbed to death by the boy.

Not far from there, Mathew Lockhart, a carpenter by trade, set up a grocery and saloon—a rough, smoke-stained place that drew miners like flies. Fights were frequent. But a few never ended.

Jack Comer was one of them. Killed in the Lockhart saloon by a man named Aaron, who brought down a cast iron scale weight on his head hard enough to split the skull. No law came for Aaron. No one even moved the body for a while. They say his blood soaked the floorboards so deep it rose through the cracks when it rained.

Another was Baldie Keeton, the town's tax man and drunk, known for pushing folks around. He was thrown out of the Lockhart saloon one night after one of his usual tirades—staggering and yelling into the dark.

He never made it home.

They found him the next morning, torn and lifeless across the railroad tracks, his limbs bent wrong, his head crushed like a melon.

Some say he fell. Others say something waited for him out there.

But not everything that died here stayed dead for long.

Some things got back up.

Wrong-shaped.

Wrong-minded.

And hungry for the ones who put them down. Even in its earliest years, travelers whispered of spook lights that blinked into existence along the tracks at night—flickering globes that hovered, pulsed, and vanished when followed.

The tracks at Hope Furnace Station where ghostly lights appear between the location of the Hope Furnace Station schoolhouse and Hope-Moonville Road.

Some said it was gas.

Others said it was the dead.

And if you believe the stories that followed...the lights were only the beginning.

Hope Furnace Station Ghost Story: The Desperate Twinkling

Nathan Brewer was known as a man of order. A farmer by trade, 56 years old, weathered by the land and quiet in speech—but beneath the calm was a perfectionist's mind. He kept his records tight, his tools sharp, and his debts cleared to the cent. Nothing out of place. Nothing forgotten.

But in the first edges of spring 1868, something broke loose. It started with a feud.

David Keeton, the county tax collector and a known brute, crooked in both law and bone, had it out for Brewer.

Brewer accused him of evading tax codes—filed it formal, by the book. But Keeton wasn't a man to be shamed, especially by someone poorer and more principled.

Keeton struck back. Filed a charge. Pressed the courts.

$250 fine. Nearly half a year's earnings were gone in ink and smirk. Brewer paid it. But Keeton wasn't finished. With friends in the courthouse and rot in his heart, he threatened more charges—more chains. He told folks he'd bury Brewer in paperwork, in fines, in jail. Said the man would die penniless and behind bars.

Brewer's answer was calm. Too calm.

"I will not be taken alive, that is for sure."

What He Left Behind

Brewer put his affairs in order like a man winding a clock. He paid off debts. Sealed ledgers. He took his son aside and handed him a box of family deeds, letters, and wills. He said to guard it well. He dressed in his Sunday coat, walked to town, and bought powder and lead.

That afternoon, he loaded his musket slow.

Not in his home. Not in his barn.

He walked down to the rail lines near Hope Furnace Station, where the tracks cut through brush and bramble like scars. The same spur where Keeton rode by once a week. And there, he put the barrel under his jaw and fired. The shot echoed off the trees like thunder.

What was left of him soaked into the ballast stones.

The perfectionist had made his final mark.

But Not Everything Was Settled

That should've been the end of it. But the woods had other plans.

Within nights, strange lights began to appear along the stretch of track where Brewer's body fell—small, flickering orbs, not like lanterns or stars. They moved with purpose near the rails almost as if following a corpse crawling. Danced in place. Crawled. Slunk.

Twinkled when no one was near.

At first, folks thought it was gas. Or tricks of the frost.

But the lights didn't drift—they pointed.

They followed walkers along the railway.

They hovered by windows.

Some said it was Nathan Brewer. That the man who tied off every detail in life had left one thing undone. Something important.

And now—he was trying to say something.

Frantic. Silent. Dragging himself along the rails.

Burning through the dark to be heard.

But no one could understand. The lights pulsed. Spun. Flickered out.

What had he forgotten?

What did he take to the grave still unfinished?

And what happens when he realizes no one's listening? Some say he still waits. Not peaceful. Not patient. A man who planned everything—except the *after*.

The No Man's Lane: Between Hope Furnace Station & Moonville

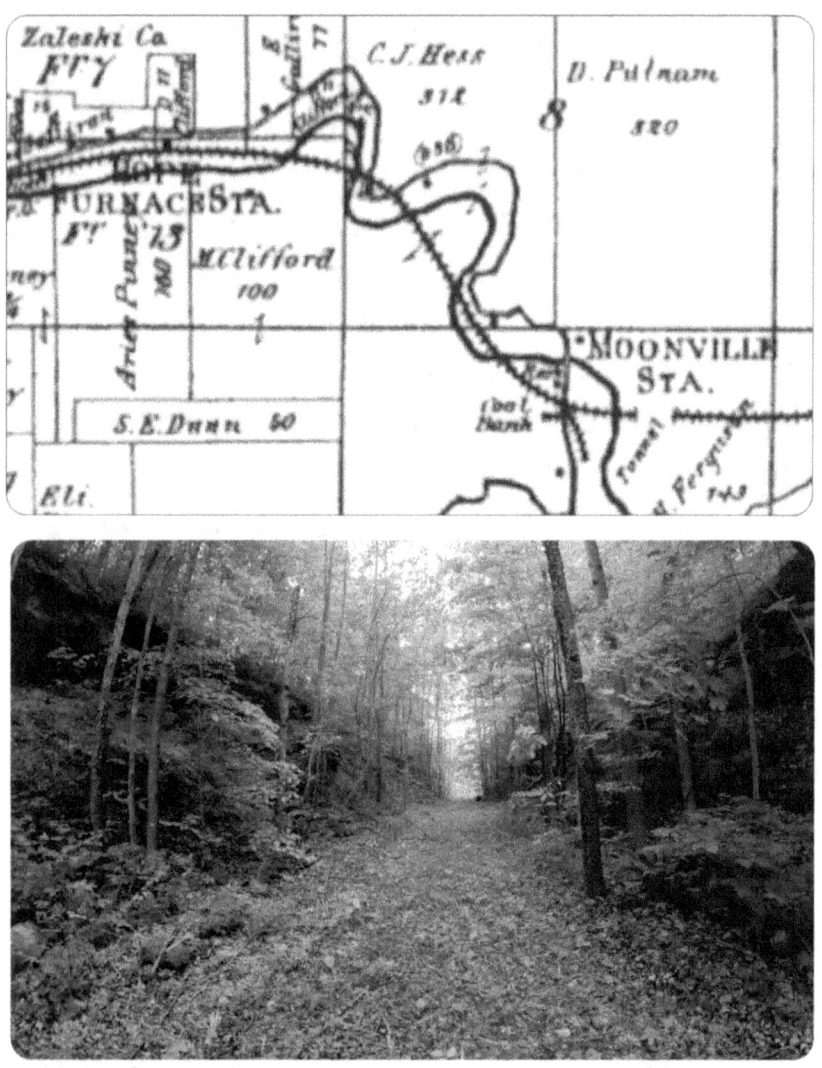

No Man's Land Between Hope Furnace Station and Moonville

There was a desolate stretch of track between Hope Furnace Station and Moonville that trainmen called no man's land. It was only a mile long.

But it was a mile they all dreaded.

Back when the line was still alive with coal and iron, this section twisted over narrow trestles above Raccoon Creek, then knifed straight through the sandstone hills. The cut had been blasted out by hand, raw and sheer. Rainwater soaked its walls. Heat cracked them. And every train that passed sent a tremor through the stone.

It didn't take much. One hairline fracture. One echo in the wrong place. And the rock would come down. There was no siding. No place to slow. No time to pray. The sound of wheels over that mile was different—duller, like something listening. Some said it wasn't just the stone that made men uneasy.

A wreck occurred in the No Man's Land. And something lingered after—

Said something else lingered there. Something left behind in the wreck. The trains are long gone now. But people still avoid that mile. And when they don't... they tend not to stay long.

No Man's Land Ghost Story: The Last God-Forsaken Ride of Red Landrum

On Monday, December 26th, 1938, the Baltimore and Ohio freight No. 88 barreled east through the ravaged woods between Moonville and Hope Furnace Station. Sixty-three cars long, double-headed, heavy with coal and freight, it roared into a night of cold rain and creeping wind.

The temperature had begun its slow spiral downward.

The first bite of a coming winter gale raked across McArthur and Athens by morning.

This was a desolate stretch of track, long abandoned by all but the trains. The boomtowns were dead. The furnaces had gone dark. Between the hollowed remnants of Mineral and the quiet streets of Zaleski, nothing stirred now but the wind in the trees and the groan of steel over stone. Civilization had rotted out of the hills. Only a few warped skeletons of houses stood, leaning in on themselves, ribs of walls showing through. The rest was forest—thick, dark, and cold. What remained of the dead lay in forgotten cemeteries, the earth sunken in places where the coffins had collapsed.

It was a place no one lived anymore.

And a place no one lingered.

At the throttle of Engine No. 1 was Charles "Red" Landrum, 54 years old. A railroad man to the bone. Born in Jackson, raised in Chillicothe, a father of three, known for his steady hands and sharp reflexes. He'd run this line before. He knew its curves, its climbs, its quiet terror. He knew how fast to take the turn near the creek, how hard to brake on the downgrades through the cut.

But he didn't know the hill had come down.

Somewhere in the early hours, a seam in the sandstone split. The freeze-thaw of winter had opened the rock like a rotten tooth, and the heavy rain had done the rest. A rockslide spilled across the tracks—wet stone and tree roots, and in the center of it, a boulder the size of a barn roof.

It had settled into the rails like something waiting.

Red saw it in the beam of the engine light.

Too late.

The train slammed into the rock at full speed. The lead engine buckled. The second jackknifed. Cars folded behind them like paper. Twelve derailed outright. Coal burst from shattered hoppers, iron from broken cars, splinters, and fire, and twisted steel all raining down together.

In the cab, Landrum was crushed.

A piece of the frame punched through his leg and held him fast. Then the boiler gave way, and scalding steam blasted through the broken cab. He was trapped. He was pinned in place as the heat stripped the flesh from his arms and face, boiled his lungs, and melted him alive in a storm of vapor and iron.

By December 28th, they had 200 men out clearing the wreck. They dragged away the mangled cars, blasted apart the stone, and patched the rail.

Red Landrum's body was recovered from the cab— broken, scalded, and nearly unrecognizable. He was sent home and buried with proper rites.

But they didn't clear everything. Not from that mile.

Something stayed in the cut.

Something that wore his shape.

Or remembered his suffering.

Some say Landrum's ghost still moves through the old cut where the rockslide happened. They say when a December storm begins to build, and the air takes on that raw bite, something shifts in the woods near the track.

Hikers report hearing the shriek of metal on metal where no train runs.

The whistle moans through the pines. A red glow shimmers in the cut where no train has passed in decades.

And then, something drags itself across the gravel when the air goes dead still.

A figure, twisted and burned, wandering the ruin of the line, searching for something he never finished.

They say the engineer never left his post.

He never finished the run.

And he doesn't plan to stop.

And if you walk that mile in the dead hush of winter—when the fog drags low and the trees hold still—you might hear it: the peel of a train horn where no engine runs.

The clatter of steel wheels on buried track.

The groan of a man who never got out.

If that sound follows you, and the air shifts cold behind your neck, don't stop.

Don't look.

Pick up your pace and pass the point where the wreck took him—because he may still be trying to finish the ride. And you may be in his way.

The Town: Moonville

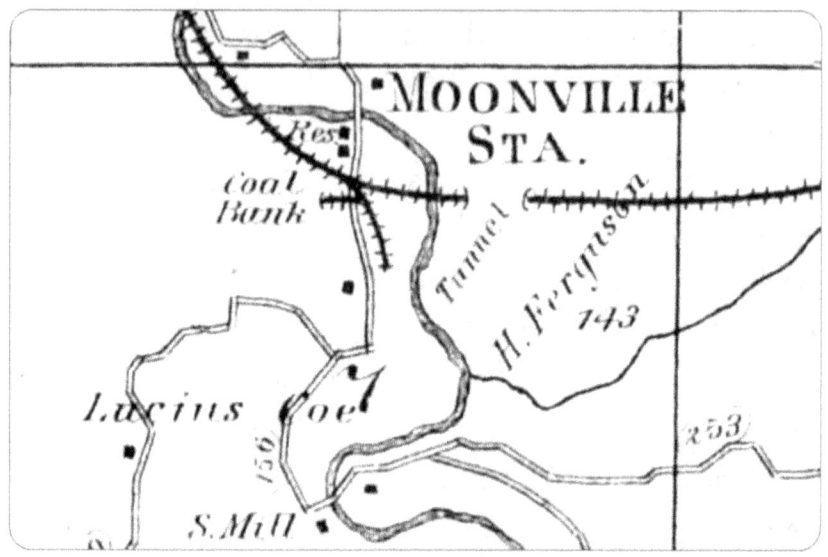

The home of Emeline and Samuel Coe

Moonville Families: The Coes

Oscar Coe—1905-06 and his sister, Bernice Coe (Dearth), on the front porch at Moonville. Image: Neil Dearth (his mother is to the left) and Alice's House, Vinton County Historical Society.

Before Moonville was a name whispered in ghost stories, it was a place carved out of the wilderness by stubborn hands. In the early 1800s, Samuel Coe (1813–1883) and his wife Emeline (1817–1895) settled deep along Raccoon Creek—far from any real road, where the forest grew thick and the sky narrowed overhead. There was no town then.

Just a path leading out from Bolin Mills, winding like a vein through the hills.

Samuel built a house and a steam sawmill down the ridge from the cemetery. Like many who carved out a living in the hills, he also put his land to work—running a farm, keeping a small grocery, and offering lodging to travelers.

1860 census showing the Coe Family: Samuel Coe (Farmer and Lumber Dealer), Emeline Coe (wife), Geo D Coe (Tends Sawmill), Mary J Coe (servant), William C Coe, Romain Coe, Preston Coe, Emma Coe, Martha E Coe, Oscar Coe, Ellen J Thomas (servant), Willington Coe, William Devore (tenant)

Coe floated logs and coal down the creek or took it by wagon path through the rugged trails—until the mid-1850s, when he and his neighbor Henry Ferguson petitioned for something permanent: a road connecting their corner of the world to the furnace town of Zaleski.

Road Notice.

NOTICE is hereby given that a petition will be presented to the Commissioners of Vinton County, Ohio, at their next session, for an order to open a road in Brown Township, in said county, commencing at Coe's Mill on Raccon Creek, thence by way of Moonville and the residence of Alonzo Ferguson, to Big Sand Furnace, being an extension of the county road leading from Boland's Mill, on said creek to Coe's Mill.

H. FERGUSON,
and other citizens of Brown Township.

July 29.—4w

The road would snake past their mill, through Moonville, down to Big Sand Station (later Hope Furnace Station), and on to Big Sand Furnace itself. What followed was a burst of iron, timber, and coal. A railway was laid—the Marietta and Cincinnati carving its line through the forest and placing a small train station on the Coe property where the trees thinned.

Kennard/Moonville Mine along the railway in Moonville. Very little remains but an indent and acid mine drainage to show the mine was once there.

A tunnel was blasted through the ridge on the neighboring Ferguson land, and in the clearing it created, the moon shone through—clear and bright, even in the densest woods. So, the place was named Moonville.

The Coe land stayed in the family for generations until the mid-1900s, when the state began swallowing up the past. The trees came back. So did the silence. Today, the Zaleski State Forest has claimed what's left.

You'll find no rooftops now, no chimneys. Just broken bricks, mossed-over fencing, and low stones that once framed homes. But the land remembers. And some say the Coes are still watching.

Moonville Families: The Fergusons

Henry and Rhoda Ferguson were among the earliest to settle in Moonville. They farmed the land, like most in the hills did back then—weather-worn hands, small plots, and just enough to get by. But as the mines opened and the railroad pushed through, the work shifted. Members of the Ferguson family took jobs underground in the local shafts, while others worked above, helping to build, maintain, or run the trains that cut through their own land. They were a large family, rooted deep in the soil and stone of Vinton County—tied to the land, the coal beneath it, and the steel that ran over it.

1860 census showing the Ferguson Family: Henry Ferguson (Farmer), Roda (wife), Joseph Clarke (Farmer), Ardella Clarke(Servant), Johannah Sales (Servant), David (Son of Farmer), William Ferguson, Levi Sales

They helped build Moonville. Their property was across from the Coes and is now managed by the Ohio Division of Forestry. But if you follow the old Hope-Moonville Road and walk the short gravel stretch toward the tunnel, watch the woods carefully. On the left, tucked behind the brush, there's a dirt path—no sign, just an old ghost of a trail.

Follow it, and you'll be walking the bones of Moonville.

Look close: you might see foundation stones, a collapsed well, or toward the tunnel, what's left of a barrel, half-sunk in the leaves.

And those barrels? They weren't for water.

During Prohibition in the 1920s, this place was quieter. Most families had already left by the 1930s, the mines gone and the tracks near empty. But not everyone was gone. The hills held onto secrets.

Folks whispered that more than souls haunted the hills—someone was distilling whiskey above the tunnel.

No one ever said who ran the stills. No one ever asked.

And sometimes, if you're out there long past dusk, you might still catch a strange scent on the wind— sweet, sharp, and burning.

Not moonlight.

Something older.

Something brewed.

Hikers pass through at dusk and feel eyes on them. Some say it's just the wind. Others say the long-dead owners of the whiskey stills keep watch—over their land, their barrels... and their secrets.

Moonville Cemetery

Known Graves:

Coe, Samuel (7/20/1813 – 4/21/1883)

Spouse: Emeline Coe.

Coe, Emeline (11/4/1817 - 11/5/1895)

Spouse: Samuel Coe

Children of Samuel and Emaline Coe
buried at Moonville:

Coe, Martha Ellen (8/20/1855 - 9/3/1863)

Inscription: I want to be an angel and with the angel stand. A crown upon my forehead and a harp within my hand.

Coe, Preston
(3/22/1847–2/28/1865)
Son of Samuel and Emaline
Coe

Coe, William Clifford "Cliff"
(6/30/1844–4/28/1899)
Died of a heart attack while holding a child (Ruth) in the Moonville Depot. Age 55.
Spouse: Lovisa Coe

Coe, Lovisa Jane Porter
(12/8/1843–2/6/1885)
Died of consumption.
Spouse: Cliff Coe

Children of Clifford and Lovisa buried at Moonville:
Coe, Jacob L. (1868–3/5/1869)
Coe, Baby (1872–1873)
Coe, William P. (1884–10/20/1884)

Coe, Wellington C.
(3/10/1824–2/28/1887)
Died from pneumonia.
Inscription:
Co C, 30th O.V.I. Civil War Veteran

Coe, Worthington (–1884) about 85 years old Co C 30 Ohio Infantry Listed as: Brother of Preston Coe

Ferguson, Charlie (October 1829–1902) brother of Henry Ferguson. Killed by a train at Moonville

Joiner, Infant Unknown

 **Jones, Benjamin Thomas** (5/22/1832–2/24/1912) Spouse: Rachel Stilwell
Jones, Rachel Josephine Stilwell (6/12/1842–4/1/1914) Spouse: Benjamin Jones

Children of Benjamin and Rachel Jones:

Jones, Louzanna M. (1862–9/14/1865) Inscription: 3 years 15 days Daughter of B. & R. Jones

 **Jones, Eber Eugene** (12/3/1875–6/30/1876) Inscription: Asleep in Jesus

Jones, Ideliae (7/5/1874–7/15/1874) Inscription: Asleep in Jesus

Mace, Grace (1877–8/24/1877)
Daughter of Hiram and Adeline Scott Mace

Mace, James -(1833–8/24/1899) Grandfather of Frank
Mace. Spouse: Martha Elizabeth Mace.

Ross, Jerry (Jeremiah) (1841–unknown died before
1880 but was still alive in 1860 census at age 20)
Uncle of Billy Ross and Brother of Newton Ross

Stilwell, Matilda (1798–3/17/1870)
Mother of William and Isaiah Jr. Stilwell
Spouse: Isaiah Stilwell

Stilwell, William
(4/20/1827–5/5/1876)

Stilwell, Sarah Ann Lentner
(10/24/1830–8/21/1905)

William Stilwell
(1827–1876)

Stilwell, Albert (1896-1900) Age 4
Choked to death on a .22 cartridge Lived at the head of
Wolf Pen Hollow. Child of Sarah Elizabeth Bowman and
Isaiah Dallas Stilwell

Stilwell, Bessie Viola (9/14/1905–10/2/1910)
Daughter of Frank and Cordelia Stilwell, Age 6.
Hot cup of coffee spilled down her back.

Thorn, Constantine (8/16/1863–10/11/1863)
Son of F.M. and S. Thorn. Aged 2 months, 26 days.

Betz, Bancrats Bamgratius Hescari (1819–4/3/1879)
Hit by a train while walking the tracks.

Betz, Christina Mondheim (1819–1872)
Bancrats' spouse

Moonville: The Bigger Picture

The road into Moonville where homes once stood by the wayside.

The town grew—soot-covered men and the steady thud of picks echoing through the hills like a heartbeat underground. Above the Kennard Mine, near the edge of the cemetery, stood a small one-room building that served as both schoolhouse and church. Children learned their letters by day and bowed their heads by lantern light at night, the sound of mining never far off.

Just down Mace Road, the Moonville Mine lay tucked into the belly of the hill, its mouth yawning black in the stone. And as the coal came out, more families came in—names like Mace, Hess, Kennard, and Pinney, written into the dust and ledger books of Moonville's brief but burning rise.

Coming down from the cemetery, the schoolhouse was located on the sharp turn here. Only foundation stones remain.

Moonville was never meant to stand alone. It was part of the bigger picture. As mining towns sprang up along the Marietta and Cincinnati Railroad—later taken over by the Baltimore and Ohio—Moonville became a point of passage.

People drifted through by foot or caught rides on the freight trains, moving from one mining camp to the next in search of work, shelter, or something they didn't yet have a name for.

There were few roads in those days. The only one followed Raccoon Creek, crawling up and down the hills, flooding out every spring.

If you wanted through, the rails were your best chance.

Moonville Tunnel when the shrill squeal of wheel to track still echoed in the hills and hollows. Image: Lori Calderon.

But the number of people on foot and the constant movement of trains across narrow cuts and high trestles came at a cost.

Image: Lori Calderon

Accidents were common.

Deaths were frequent.

And over time, Moonville became known not only as a hub—but as a place where the dead didn't always stay buried. Some said the woods watched.

Others said the tracks remembered.

And more than once, someone walking alone through the tunnel swore they weren't alone.

Moonville Tunnel holds nothing but silence today—and the dead.

For years, Moonville held its place as a quiet hub in the wilderness—isolated, but woven into something larger. A small town in a long shadow. It remains—abandoned by the living, occupied by the past.

Moonville Ghost Story: The Ghost of Moonville

Where It All Began

People always ask where it started—where Moonville Tunnel got its ghosts, what opened the door and let them in. There are plenty of stories out there, most of them made up. But this one... this one's real. It's old, passed down by folks who lived and died in the hills around Moonville. A tragedy so fierce and senseless it may have cracked something wide open.

A scar in the tracks. And it never healed.

The Wreck

In the late 1800s, the forests between Zaleski and Athens were stitched with mining camps—small towns clinging to the lifeblood of the Marietta & Cincinnati Railroad. Moonville was one of them. Just a few families in the center—like the Fergusons, who farmed and worked the rails, and the Coes, who ran a sawmill, coal mine, and the depot.

One set of tracks cut through it all for both eastbound and westbound trains. There was no room for mistakes. Telegraph lines connected station to station, and it was up to the dispatchers to keep trains from colliding—watching signals, directing traffic, warning crews.

Usually, it worked.

But on November 4, 1880, it didn't.

That day, the eastbound train rolled through southern Ohio with 37-year-old Engineer Theodore Lawhead at the helm. The westbound was coming straight toward him, but no message warned of its approach. On a blind curve just a half mile from Moonville Tunnel, the two engines collided.

The hillside shook with the crash.

Iron screamed.

Cars tore apart.

Fires flashed from the torn boilers, black with coal smoke.

Lawhead died instantly.

So did his fireman, Charles Krick, just 25 years old.

His body was blown apart by steam pressure. Lawhead was mangled beyond recognition—crushed under iron, limbs shattered, his last breath buried beneath the weight of the machine he ran.

After that, Moonville was never the same.

The First Ghost

The collision left more than wreckage. It left a stain.

Soon after, trainmen began refusing to ride that stretch of track alone. They said something waited near the tunnel—just beyond the curve where the crash happened.

Said they saw a light, small and flickering, high on the bluff.

At first, it looked like a warning—a signal of danger ahead. Then it moved.

The light floated down the rock face in complete silence, drifting toward the rails. And as it settled in the center of the track, men began to see something more:

A pale figure draped in white.

There was a halo of twinkling lights around its head.

Eyes wide. Red. Bulging.

A lantern swinging from one hand.

It didn't move. It didn't speak.

It just stood there.

And then, just before the train reached it—gone.

No one called him anything back then.

They didn't have to.

They knew who it was.

Theodore Lawhead.

The engineer who never saw the warning.

Now, forever giving one.

They say he was the first.

The one who tore the veil.

The ghost that opened Moonville Tunnel to whatever came after. And even before.

And some nights, especially in November—when the wind cuts deeper, and sleet rattles through the trees like teeth—people still hear it.

The phantom roar of a train that never arrives.

A burst of cold from nowhere.

And then... a light.

Dangling in the air.

Swinging, waiting.

Just above the tracks.

As if someone still stands there, trying to signal the living.

Or warn them.

Too late.

The area of the wreck is a half mile from the tunnel, near the first wooden trestle at the blind curve. This is where the Ghost of Moonville is seen. On the anniversary of the wreck, I met with some folks who joined me on a paranormal investigation at the site of the accident.

We heard voices. I asked, "Are you dead?"

A voice answered, "Yes, I am, right?"

Another answered, "Yeah, you got squashed."

I asked, "Do you still walk the tracks?"

The answer, "Forever."

At the time the wreck, a huge gust of wind nearly blew down the tripods. That same night, we heard several times, the gusty roar of ghost train on tracks. And after asking the spirits to blow the horn, a haunting wail swept through.

WEATHER INDICATIONS.

LOCAL:—Barometer. sunset. 29:35; sunrise
29:40; noon. 29:44; thermometer, sunset. 35;
sunrise. 32; noon, 30; wind sunset. north-
west; sunrise, north-west; noon, north.
STATE—Clear and slightly colder.

The ghost of Moonville, after an absence of one year, has returned and is again at its old pranks, haunting B. & O. S.-W. freight trains and their crews.

Monday night the ghost appeared just east of the cut, which is one half mile the other side of Moonville. It showed up in front of fast freight No.99 west bound, which is due at Moonville at 8:50 p. m. The train was hauled by engine 226, in charge of Engineer William Washburn. The conductor was Mr. Charles Bazler.

The ghost was attired in a pure white robe, and carried a lantern. It had a flowing white beard, its eyes glistened like balls of fire, and surrounding it was a halo of twinkling stars. As the train approached, the lantern was swung across the track. Engineer Washburn gave the proper whistle signal, and stopped the train. As he did so, his ghostship stepped off the track and disappeared amidst the rocks near by.

This is not the first time the same ghost has stopped and delayed trains. It has been at that business, off and on, since the frightful collision at that point, in which Engineer Lawhead lost his life and Engineer Wash Walters was injured.

Chillicothe Gazette Chillicothe, Ohio · Wednesday, January 23, 1895

Moonville Ghost Story: Lavender Lady

Where Spirits Linger

When people join me on my night hikes and ghost hunts along the Moonville Rail Trail, I rarely have time to tell every spirit's story. We pass by places where lives ended hard—places where the dead still walk.

The rail cuts through a graveyard of forgotten souls—miners, trackwalkers, brakemen, lovers, drunkards, and strangers who never made it home.

The railway was the only path through these hills, and in the years when the coal ran, and the signals failed, people met steel far too often.

Some left behind only blood on the ballast.

The result? A long history of apparitions that now haunt this old but renewed rail path. Those who once called this place home handed down their stories, and I pass them on—to anyone willing to listen. One of them is about a gentle, sweet-natured old woman whose legend still lingers in the woods.

And she deserves to be remembered.

The Woman on the Tracks

She lived in a house just inside the bounds of Hope Furnace Station. An old woman. Quiet. Spry. Known by her walk and the sweet scent of lavender perfume.

She traveled the tracks to see her kin or buy groceries. Every week. No matter the weather. She moved carefully, feet between the ties, arms tucked in tight, passing trestles and tunnels with the patience of someone who knew the trains and feared them.

But not enough.

One winter day, the engine came on faster than expected—maybe fog, maybe snow, maybe the old woman simply didn't hear it.

She was spry for her age. But not spry enough.

She was struck.

Hard.

And the train didn't stop.

Couldn't.

Not fast enough.

The wreck crew found her shawl snagged on the front coupler. And they found her body later—what was left of it—dragged from the hillside clear to the Moonville Tunnel.

Her bones were broken and ground across the gravel. Her head, they whispered, had turned more than once. The rails had eaten through the wool of her dress, her skin, and finally her shape.

After that, she never left.

She walks the line still—

Through the deep pockets of forest.

Across the splintering trestles that groan above the creek.

And always, always through the tunnel.

Not fast.

Not angry.

Just… endless.

People who see her don't hear her footsteps.

They catch a certain fragrance first.

The Scent That Stayed

Back then, folks didn't bathe like they do now—once a week, maybe less. Instead, women dabbed scented oils on kerchiefs, tucked them into their dresses, or rubbed fragrant salves into their joints to soothe old pains. The old woman, it's said, favored lavender. She wore it that day, maybe for her elbows. Perhaps just to feel decent. But when the train took her, it mixed that sweet scent with the reek of iron, steam, and burned skin.

Still Walking

Now, those who walk the trail after dark sometimes catch it—not a hint, not a whisper, but a wave—thick and cloying, like something spilled in the cold.

It rolls out of the tunnel just before she does.

Her shape appears, back bowed, walking the ties like always.

But she never makes it past the far end.

She just vanishes.

But the scent lingers.

And so does the thought... that she's still trying to get somewhere.

Still trudging through the dark with lavender on her skin and death at her heels.

Moonville Ghost Story: The Bully

The Keeton family once held respect in the hills near Hope Furnace. They were well-liked, dependable, and rooted in the land.

But even good trees bear rotten fruit.

David "Baldie" Keeton was the black rot in the Keeton name.

A farmer by trade. A tax collector by appointment. A drunk and a brute by reputation.

He was known across Vinton County for his cruelty. He beat his wife. He terrorized his children. He turned every room cold when he entered it. At sixty-five years old, in the summer of 1886, Baldie was still a towering hulk of a man—broad-shouldered, thick-legged, and mean as ever. The years hadn't softened him.

If anything, they'd sharpened his temper.

Locals said you could hear his voice before you saw him—low, snarling, always looking to provoke. He had a habit of targeting the smallest man in the room, casting insults and tossing little things like pebbles at them until fists were raised. But he didn't fight with punches—he used brute force, wrapping men in crushing embraces until they collapsed, breathless and broken.

He lived just outside Moonville, near Hope Furnace Station. Nobody wanted to be his neighbor.

Few dared stand against him.

The Night of the Brawl

On the evening of June 26, 1886, Baldie returned from Zaleski, where he'd appeared in court on a civil complaint. He was furious, fueled by anger and liquor, and wandered into the local tavern to stew in both.

He started another fight.

The barkeep had seen enough. Baldie was told to leave. When he refused, two men hauled him outside.

He never came back through the door. At first, his wife assumed he'd passed out in a ditch or taken shelter with family. But when the second night passed without word, she sent out men to search the rail line between Zaleski and Hope Furnace.

They found him on the tracks.

Or what was left of him.

His body had been mutilated, twisted across the rails, limbs bent and unrecognizable. The skin was split open along his back and legs. The head—barely still attached— was flattened on one side like a crushed melon.

The coroner claimed he'd been struck by a train.

But the townsfolk whispered what they suspected: he was dead long before the engine hit him.

The newspaper tried to make it palatable:

"David Keeton, an old resident of Hope Furnace and well-known all over the county, was found dead Sunday morning, June 27, on the railroad, halfway between Hope Station and Zaleski. Mr. Keeton was in Zaleski all day Saturday, engaged in a lawsuit, and when he left town along in the night to go home, he had just time enough to meet the midnight express going west, and it is generally supposed that this was the train that ran over him; however, trains were running all night, and probably several trains passed over him, as he was found in the morning horrible mangled."

But no one mourned. Not really.

They buried him without ceremony.

The Ghost in the Gravel

Not long after, children were warned to stay away from the tracks from Zaleski to Moonville Tunnel.

Not because of trains.

Because of him.

Some say he walks the rails still—hulking, slouched, his head lolling unnaturally to one side.

His boots drag in the gravel. His voice comes low and dripping with anger, grumbling like it did when he was eager for a fight.

He's been seen above the tunnel, standing like a statue on the ridge.

Still. Watching.

And then the rocks begin to fall.

Small at first. Then larger.

Those who walk the path below have felt stones strike their shoulders. When they look up, no one is there—just the black shape of the tunnel and the wind pushing through.

Some believe it's Baldie, trapped in death with the same rage he carried in life.

Still looking to provoke.

Still hungry for pain.

Still haunting the rails that he died on.

And still looking for a fight.

Moonville Ghost Story: The Brakeman's Bottle

In the early days of the railroad, before air brakes and electric signals, trains were slowed by men who climbed atop the moving cars, clung to the roof, and turned handbrakes by muscle and grit alone.

They were called brakemen.

Their work was hell.

Up ladders, across slick roofs, jumping from car to car as the train thundered beneath them.

Rain turned the roof to glass. Snow turned it to death. And if they didn't duck fast enough—a tunnel roof would take off their skull like a dandelion head, after puffing off the flying seeds, is popped from the stem.

Brakemen didn't last long. Most turned to whiskey. It numbed the hands. It stilled the nerves.

It softened the nightmares.

But sometimes, it got them killed.

The Sleep

One night, a brakeman was walking the line from Zaleski to Moonville, bottle in hand, the moonlight cutting across the tracks in long, pale ribbons.

He drank.

And walked.

And drank.

His boots scuffed the stones. His lantern burned low. And somewhere near the mouth of the tunnel, with the creek whispering just out of sight, he grew tired.

He stretched himself out—rail for a pillow, ties for a bed— and slept.

But the rails are not kind to the sleeping.

The Train Came

No one knows what time it came through. Only that it came fast, barreling toward Moonville, blowing steam and steel. The engineer never saw him.

The brakeman never felt it. The train caught his neck like a blade. His head snapped clean off, flung into the darkness, over the rail, and down the ravine where the creek roared from recent rain.

His body folded the other way—flung into the brush like a rag.

And his bottle?

It spun in the center of the tracks—around, and around— and came to rest upright.

Not a drop spilled.

The Voice That Claimed It

At dawn, a miner from Moonville trudged toward Zaleski, boots heavy with mud, when he spotted the bottle— sitting perfectly still on the iron rail.

"What a find," he muttered, reaching for it with a wide grin.

Just as his fingers touched the glass, a voice rasped out of the silence.

"That's mine."

The miner jerked back. His eyes swept the woods— left, right—nothing but trees and wind.

And then he saw it.

The blood.

Little black specks dried on the trackbed. He followed the trail—over the rail and into the thick of the brush. Pushed the brambles aside.

And there it was.

The body.

Laid out neat, arms limp, coat soaked dark.

But no head.

Just a ragged stump, crawling with flies.

The head was never found.

The Bottle That Waits

The miner left it behind. Most people did.

The bottle sat for years in the center of the track, washed by rain, warmed by sun, gathering dust and dread.

Whenever someone reached down to claim it, that voice returned—harsh, raspy, angry.

"That's mine."

Hands recoiled. Legs ran. Nobody argued.

They say the brakeman's spirit walks the line still—headless, searching the brush, the creek, the tunnel mouth—looking for whatever piece of him the train took away.

But he always knows where the bottle is.

And he's never letting it go.

So if you ever hike the Moonville Rail Trail and spot an old bottle resting quiet on the stones—think twice before you pick it up.

Especially if you live far from here.

Because folks do take it.

But they never keep it.

No matter where they set it—on a shelf, a windowsill, tucked away in some far-off corner of the house—it always speaks.

And sometime in the dead hush of night, just as the world forgets to breathe, a voice calls out from the dark:

"That's mine."

Moonville Ghost Story: Erastus Dexter Don't Know He's Dead

The Escape

Tom Dexter had run under the cover of night, his breath sharp in the cold air, his legs torn by thorns and brush. He was no more than twenty when he escaped bondage in Virginia during the Civil War.

By the time he reached the Ohio River, five bloodhounds were behind him, close enough that he could hear their feet breaking frozen leaves.

Only he made it across.

Locals say the dogs either drowned or simply vanished at the river's edge as if something older than man had called them off.

The Marriage

Tom built a new life near Ingham Station, just east of where the Moonville rails cut the forest. He lived as a free man, working the land with a quiet pride. In time, his old sweetheart from the South came north and found him. Her name was Hannah. She married him not long after.

They raised a family. One of their sons, Erastus Dexter, grew up in the hills between Mineral and Waterloo. He was known by everyone who rode the rails or drank in the town saloons—often quiet, always working. In his later years, he moved on to Nelsonville and then deeper into the coal towns.

The mines and the hard-scrabble life of the working folks around the time of the Great Depression had a way of calling men back.

The Fall

By the winter of 1929, Erastus was sixty-one and still working the seams. A collapse took him while he was deep in a McConnelsville shaft, buried under broken timber and earth. His body was recovered days later, already stiff and disfigured, and brought back across state lines to be buried in the cemetery at New Marshfield.

It should have ended there.

But in the weeks that followed, the stories began.

The Walk

At first, it was whispers—railroad men and passersby who claimed they saw a figure out near the line, walking alone just before dark. They said he wore old clothes, dusted with coal, and looked as solid as any living man. He always whistled a song. One even called out to him, thinking he was real, and the man turned, his lips still pursed as if interrupted in his tune.

He was headed toward the tunnel near Moonville. Always westbound.

It didn't take long before the name was spoken.

Erastus Dexter.

Dead but walking.

The Ghost Who Didn't Know He Was Dead

They say he never realized he died. One local said, "I seen him one night coming down off the track. He just walked past me like I wasn't there, like he's headin' home and don't know he's dead. He was just whistling away."

His path runs the line between Ingham and Moonville, sometimes farther, all the way back to where the land still remembers him. He carries no lantern. Makes no sound. But those who see him say he's as sharp and living as he ever was—until the moment he's gone. He doesn't haunt the mine where he died, nor the cemetery where his bones lie buried.

He haunts the place where he ran wild and free as a boy. Where he stole his first kiss. Where he drank warm beer on a summer night. Where the soil still knows his name. The place he loved the best. Where the past never left. And neither did he.

Moonville Ghost Story: Rabbit Days

Did you know that saying "Rabbit, rabbit" on the first day of the month is supposed to bring good luck?

Most people don't know where the phrase came from—just something whispered by grandmothers, scrawled in old farmer's almanacs, muttered under their breath before the coffee boils. But here in the hills, the saying runs older than most believe.

Some say it began after the publication of Alice in Wonderland in 1865—a strange little book where a girl follows a rabbit into another world.

Others trace it to an entry from Notes and Queries in 1909, where a man wrote of his daughter standing by the hearth, calling "Rabbit!" up the chimney on the first of each month.

If it was the first word spoken that day, it would bring a gift.

Or luck. Or protection.

But the old mining hollows remember more than books do. And sometimes, so do the dead.

The Voice in the Tunnel

One summer night, I led a small group into Moonville Tunnel—a place choked with soot and silence, where even the wind seems to walk on tiptoe.

We were doing a ghost hunt.

Nothing touristy—just lanterns, recorders, and a spirit box.

If you're unfamiliar, a spirit box scans radio frequencies in reverse. The idea is that spirits—if they have anything left to say—can use the white noise to push a word through.

Just one. Sometimes two. A lot of times, more.

Sometimes nothing.

That night, the group was quiet. No jokes. No jitters. The tunnel pressed in around us like a lung that had stopped breathing. Someone asked, "Do you like hanging around here?"

And clear as a bell came the voice, low and worn thin:

"I've got more rabbit days."

We stood frozen, unsure if we'd heard it right.

Rabbit days?

Something That Shouldn't Speak

At first, I thought it was nonsense. But something about the voice—it wasn't playful. It wasn't warm. It was empty, like someone remembering something they no longer understood. And it wasn't asking for help.

It was counting.

Later that night, I looked it up. The "rabbit, rabbit" phrase. The tradition. The superstition.

And the idea stuck with me: more rabbit days.

In the old tongue, that meant more good days than bad. Days when the crops didn't fail. When the mines held. When no one died.

Days when the ghosts stayed quiet.

But this was a ghost counting them. Still. Long after death.

And Now I Am

Maybe it didn't mean anything.

Just a blip. A coincidence.

But on the first day of the month, in the middle of Moonville Tunnel,

A ghost said something.

Clear as day.

"I've got more rabbit days."

And ever since, I can't help but wonder:

Did it mean it got lucky?

Did it mean it was happy here?

Or maybe—It was just trying to tell us it remembered.

So now, when the first of the month rolls around and if I'm near the tunnel, I say it out loud, like the old stories say to do.

Rabbit, rabbit.

Not for luck.

But just in case it's listening.

A Ghost Story for the Trail: Bloody Bones

In the Appalachian hills, where rust stains, the creeks, and iron dust hangs in the air like ash, mining families wandered from camp to camp, chasing whatever pay could be clawed from the earth. They packed up what little they had—shovels, quilts, tinware—and dragged their children behind them like shadows.

But they carried more than tools.

They carried stories.

Tales told in whispers. Rough-edged folklore passed down like quilts too worn to warm. Some were meant to keep children close. Others were darker—meant to keep children in line with warnings that lingered long after the sun went down. One such tale still clings to the hollows between Hope Furnace and Mineral City.

It's the story of a thing that waits for children who forget their prayers… and for grown folks who should've known better than to leave the door unlocked, walk past dark places alone, or break the old rules—passed down for a reason.

The Cellars and the Silence

Along the old Marietta and Cincinnati Railroad, homesteads sprouted like weeds near the rails. Each had a root cellar—either dug beneath the house or built of stone into the hillside—to store canned goods and keep them cold like a refrigerator.

But these were not just cellars.

They were mouths.

And something lived inside them.

Something red.

And wet. And wrong.

It had no skin. Its muscles twitched raw across bone, slick with pus and gleaming rot. It had no head upon its neck—not anymore. It carried that ghastly, bloody noggin in both hands, twisting it to see around corners and under shelves. The grin never faded. Teeth like old fenceposts. Eyes like rotten grapes.

They called it Bloody Bones. Or Rawhead.

And if you ever said his name out loud, it was said you cracked something open. A door. A wall. A lock. Something that let him hear you.

Shhh.

He listened for footsteps down cellar stairs—children sent for a Mason jar of pickled eggs or peaches.

He listened through the grates at night, holding his head to the floorboards above, ear tilted for whispered prayers before bed.

And if he didn't hear them…he came upstairs.

He slid beneath beds and waited for the slow rhythm of breath, for bare feet to dangle just inches above the floor.

Then—he took a bite.

A nibble, small and playful.

Just the toe. At first.

The Girl Who Asked for Company

They say that once, near the rust-streaked hollers, there was a girl left home alone too often.

Her daddy worked the night shift at the mines.

Or went out drinking.

Her mama strayed down the tracks to a friend's house to chat for hours.

Or went out drinking.

Before leaving, they'd lock the cabin door and say: "Don't talk to nobody. Don't let nobody in."

And then they'd vanish down the trail. The girl would sit in her little chair by the hearth, listening to the wind clawing at the walls.

And one night, with the fire burning low and the silence pressing in, she whispered into the dark:

"I wish someone would come play with me."

From beneath the floorboards—

Or the cellar—

Or under the stairs—

Came a voice:

"I'm coming soon."

She blinked. The flames crackled.

The shadows didn't move, but something inside them… listened.

Later, lonely again, she asked once more: "Won't someone come play with me?"

The answer was closer. "I'm almost there."

She sat in her rocking chair, the stillness now thick and warm. The air had weight. She looked to the stairs.

And when she asked a third time, it answered.

Not with words.

But with a sound:

thump

thump

thump-thump-thump

A head rolled down the stairs. Raw. Red. Grinning. Eyeless. Its teeth scraped the wooden steps as it bounced to her feet.

Then it rose.

A neck with no head. A body like a butcher's waste. Skinless. Swollen. Holding its head up high like a lantern.

The girl tried to be brave. Like the stories said.

"What long fingernails you have," she whispered.

"To scratch you with," it said.

"What big red eyes you have."

"To see you in the dark."

"And what big teeth you have."

The grin widened.

"To eat you up with."

What They Found

When her parents returned, the cabin door was still locked. The fire still burned. The chair still rocked. But their daughter was gone.

Only a small, wet pile of bones remained at the foot of the stairs.

Still warm.

They buried what was left by the creek.

They never said her name again.

And now, even today, if you're alone in those hollers…

If the wind dies down and the silence gets heavy…

Don't say you're lonely. Don't say it out loud.

Because you might hear it: "I'm coming soon."

Along the Moonville Rail Trail, scattered homes once clung to the edges of the hollows between Moonville and Mineral. Each had its root cellar—brick and mortar, cool and damp, tucked into the earth like buried mouths. They stored canned peaches, pickled eggs, and salted meat.

They also stored something else. For a time.

But the homes are gone now. Caved in. The cellars collapsed. Brick turned to dust. The wells filled with earth.

And yet...Bloody Bones didn't die.

It doesn't rot. It doesn't sleep.

So where did it go?

Some say it crept farther down the line. Found new shelter. A place just as dark. Just as hollow—the trestles and bridges over Raccoon Creek and Hewett Fork. Cool and shadowed underneath. With boards overhead where the living still walk.

Big feet. Little feet.

Some who forget their prayers.

Some who drop their candy wrappers.

Some who laugh too loud, not knowing they're being watched.

Now, when night settles thick as coal smoke, Bloody Bones stirs. One hand gripping the wooden rail.

The other clutching his slick, smiling head.

He presses it upward—just high enough to see through the cracks. And he waits. For a lull in the chatter.

For the silence between steps.

For the moment, a foot slips too close to the edge.

Then he reaches up—Quick. Wet. Certain.

And drags them down into the dark, which never ends. So, if you walk the Moonville Trail after sundown...say your prayers. Mind your feet. And whatever you do—don't look between the boards.

A Ghost Story for the Road: Hanging Rock

Out beyond the ghost town of Moonville if you keep going past Mace Road, where the trees lean in, and the dusk settles heavy, there runs a narrow gravel lane slippery as a slug—Township Road 1.

It climbs hard through the hills, winding upward, upward until it seems to float above the hollow below. The edge drops off quick—no rails, no shoulder, just air, and a long way down.

It's an old road. Older than the rail.

And it remembers what the forest forgets.

And along that road, there's a stone.

A jagged monolith jutting from the earth like a bone too big to bury.

Hanging Rock

They call it Hanging Rock now.

In Ohio's early days, when wolves still cried through the black pines, and settlers counted their dead by winter's end, the Kennedy family took shelter beneath that rock. One bitter night, chased by a starving pack, they lit fires around its base to drive back the snapping jaws and flashing teeth. The rock kept them safe.

But fire doesn't banish everything.

There is a worse story. One that came later.

One, they didn't speak so loud.

Once, a great black oak stood beside that stone—a crooked thing with gnarled limbs and bark like burned hide. And from one of its lowest branches, a man hanged himself. No one knows why.

Maybe a miner who lost his grip on the world.

Maybe a killer trying to beat the rope that waited in town.

Or maybe something darker urged him up into those limbs.

Whatever the reason, he swayed there for days—his body bloated and split, eyes plucked by birds, blackened feet tapping gently against the trunk.

He hung until someone happened by and screamed.

He Returns

They cut him down. Buried what was left.

The tree is long gone. But it never forgot.

And neither did the rock.

After that, anyone passing by after sundown—especially alone—would see him.

Not whole. Not rotted.

But swaying.

A silhouette of a man still hanging, limbs too long, body too still, rocking side to side on a rope that wasn't there. He'd hang in the air even when there was no wind. Cast a shadow even when the moon was gone.

Some say you can still hear the creak of the rope if you get too close.

Others swear they've seen the shadow twist, turning toward them.

The locals gave the place a name.

Hanging Rock.

And even now, when the dusk sets wrong, and the pines go quiet…it's best not to linger too long.

Because not every shadow wants to stay on the rock.

The Town: Ingham Station

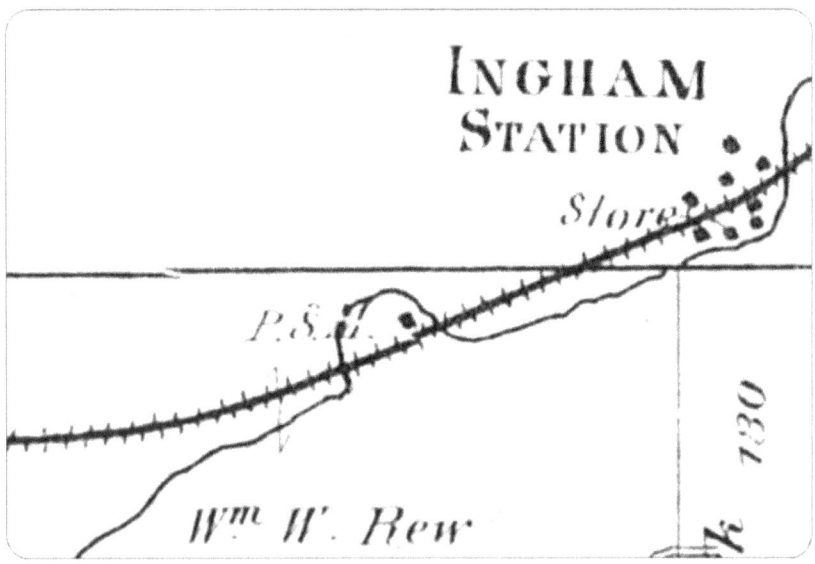

Today, little remains of Ingham Station, which once had 8 to 10 homes, a station, and a grocery store. The train path is still visible, along with an overgrown road. Initially marked as P.S.M. on the map, this station was located on Rew land and was originally known as Rew Station when the railroad was first extended. Much of the surrounding community developed around the coal mines up the tracks. While the living community may be gone, spirits still linger.

Before the ghost stories begin, you have to understand the land.

Ingham Station was once just a flicker of coal smoke and lantern light along the railroad that curled through Bear Hollow like a black snake. It was never a big town—eight or ten homes at most—but it had a depot, a store, and a one-room schoolhouse tucked behind a hill to thwart the constant roar of trains where the children of miners traced their letters by oil lamp.

The tracks here follow Hewett Fork, a stream that runs shallow beneath the trees through the long and dark Rew Forest. Where the water pools wider at the far end of the hollow—just past the bend when walking from Moonville—there was once a small station stop. Now, there's only silence, broken by the wind or the soft plunk of water dripping from the hillside.

The names are mostly gone now, but a few remain in memory and stone: Dexter. Rew. Brooks. Clark. Ingham. They were the ones who called this place home when the mines were alive. More than a couple of drifters passed through this place—men with coal dust in their teeth and names nobody remembered. Some stayed long enough to work a shift or two in the mines before vanishing down the tracks.

The Dexters were known to take them in when no one else would. There was a small outbuilding on their farm, rough-built and leaning, where the transients could sleep a night or two out of the rain. No questions asked.

Just a cot. A roof.

And whatever haunted them kept outside the door.

The Mines and the Hollow

The Ingham Mines sat at the far end of Bear Hollow, tucked deep in the shadow of the ridge. From the tracks, the old roadbeds can still be found if you know where to look—rutted, overgrown, winding like veins toward the ruins of the shafts. Some say they've seen strange lights along the old road—dim, flickering, and unsteady, like lanterns swinging in tired hands. They bump and sway through the trees, following the ruts where wagons once rolled, as if the men who labored in the dark still haven't laid down their tools.

Ghosts of workers, trudging home after a long day's haul.

Or maybe still trying to reach the mine.

Either way, they never stop. A few foundations linger along the slope, too stubborn to sink.

The remains of the abandoned schoolhouse. Foundation stones, pieces of the stove, parts of old school desks, and sometimes, the giggles of ghostly children.

The Ingham Mine is a short detour from the Zaleski Backpack Trail, located in an ancient, nameless hollow off Bear Hollow. Although the road that once led to the mine is now abandoned, it is still visible above the waters of Bear Hollow. Ghostly lantern lights are seen bobbing its path by those walking the trails.

On the other side of the second hill lie the Mineral Mines. Their buildings have collapsed into the forest floor and the openings gated shut, the boards soft with rot and carpeted in moss. But when the mist is thick, it's said the outline of those places sharpens. As if the land itself hasn't let go.

The ridge between them—the divide between Ingham and Mineral—is steep and narrow. And at night, it carries sounds.

Echoes that don't match any living step. Because here, ghosts did thrive. And still do!

Ingham Ghost Story: The Lost Hand

Payday and Whiskey

Allen Allbaugh and his brother had spent too many years under the coal dust. They walked daily between Zaleski and Luhrig, a long, brutal stretch nearly nine miles one way. When they were lucky, they caught the train—the Baltimore & Ohio as it came grinding through the town, and with a quick dash and a firm grip, they'd hoist themselves aboard.

That late summer evening in 1907, they got off shift early. The sun was still high, the air thick with gnats and heat. It was payday.

Allen bought a bottle. Said he was owed something smooth after all the jagged days.

They didn't have long. Not more than a few sips before they heard it—the whistle. The train was early. The Baltimore & Ohio was already screaming down the line, iron shaking the ground. Both men burst out the door of the saloon and ran for it, Allen clutching the neck of the whiskey bottle in one hand like it was his last possession on earth. Some say they saw him smiling.

The Fall

The train slowed near Luhrig. Allen's brother jumped off. Rolled hard but got up. Looked back.

No Allen.

At first, no one worried. Allen's leg had never been right—not since a fall of coal at Luhrig lamed his foot. He limped worse when he drank. People figured he missed the jump or took a slower road home.

But by dusk, he hadn't come back. And by the next morning, the family knew something was wrong. They sent men out with lanterns, combing the tracks and hollows between Bear Hollow and Ingham Station. Nothing.

The Body in the Brush

It was days later, under the sweltering stink of August, when two men walking the rails caught a sour stench rising from the brush. They thought it was a rotting deer.

They were wrong.

It was Allen.

Or what was left of him.

His body was bloated, blackened, and picked at by animals. Maggots covered what was left. And his hand—the one that had clutched the bottle—was gone. Torn clean. The wound had crusted with dirt and flies. They buried what they found in a plain wooden box and didn't say much after.

But the hand did not turn up right away.

Not with the body. Not with the grave.

Weeks later, someone found it.

Not the whole thing. Just bone, sinew, and glass shards nestled in the weeds outside Moonville Tunnel. The fingers were curled as if still holding something.

They said Allen must have caught the train's edge drunk, slow, and limping—held tight to the car with his good hand, whiskey in the other. That arm jutted out when the train barreled into the narrow stone throat of Moonville Tunnel.

And the tunnel took it. Tore it. Swallowed it.

Left him bleeding and screaming until he fell.

The Tracks He Walks

Not long after the burial, people started seeing something near Ingham Station. A figure walking the rails at dusk, limping heavily. He wore work clothes blackened by earth and sweat. His eyes were wide, unsure. Like someone who woke up and didn't know where he was.

When folks got close, he'd turn. Raise one arm.

Show the stump. And vanish.

They say it was Allen. Still walking the stretch he died on. He is still looking for what he lost.

Not the bottle. Not the train.

The hand. It was never buried properly.

And he won't rest 'til it is.

The Hand

So, if you're walking the line near Bear Hollow at sundown, and you hear the wind whimper through the ties...don't stop.

Don't look back.

And don't offer your hand to anyone who asks.

Because Allen is still out there.

And he's not looking for company.

He's looking for a match.

But so, too, is his hand—still crawling.

Still searching.

Looking for something to attach to.

It might find you.

Here is how a couple of locals told the story—

Mike Shea

Bill Price was a state park naturalist, and part of his job was interviewing and collecting information about the people and culture in Moonville and Lake Hope. In an interview, resident Mike Shea recounted the discovery of Albaugh's body in this way: -

"Allan Albaugh was drinking and hopped a train at Zaleski with a jug of whiskey. No one heard from him. They found him dead this side of Ingham near Bear Hollow. Mike Shea smelled him one day and Frank McWhorter and a one-eyed fellow found him when attracted by the smell. He was full of maggots, been dead several days."

The Town: King's Station

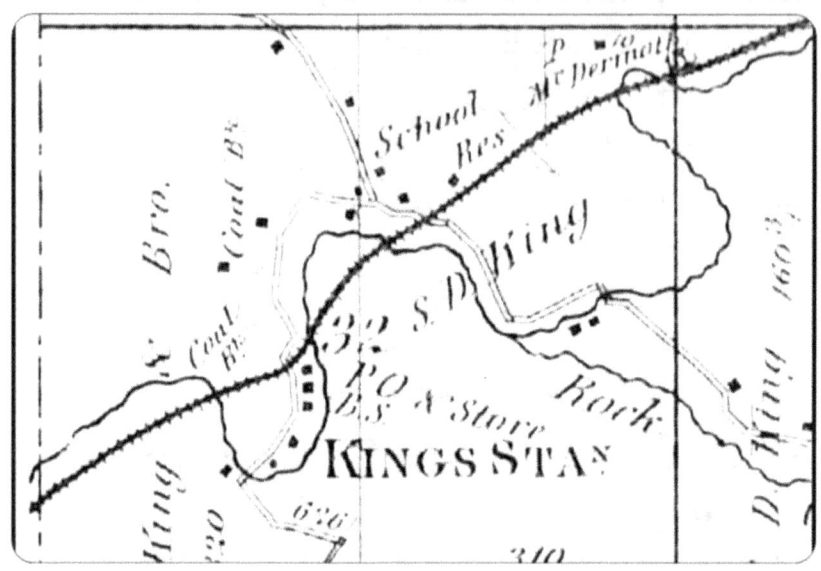

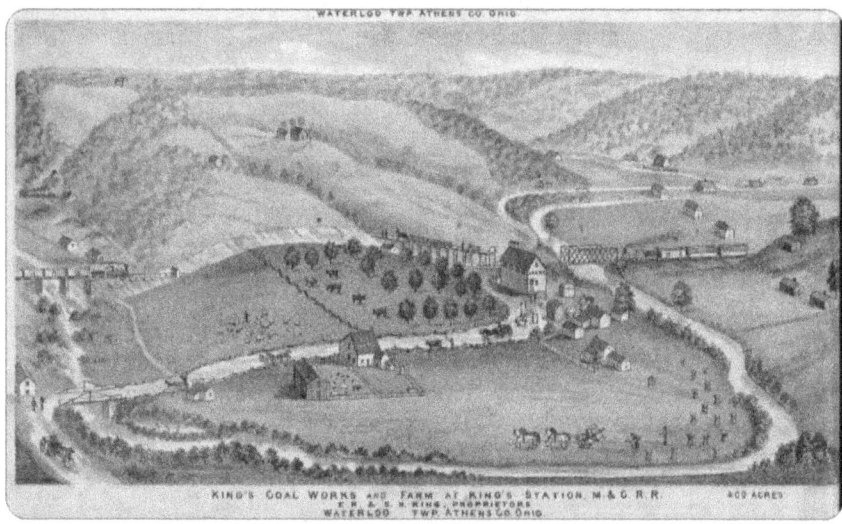

When the railroad came cutting through the hills, it wasn't just iron and smoke it brought—it stitched together land that had long stood apart. Isolated farms and forgotten hollows were suddenly bound to the rest of the world by steel and steam.

Some landowners saw what was coming. They gave the rail line right-of-way across their property—not out of charity, but foresight. A train meant connection. And connection meant money.

The King family cashed in on it.

The last home still on the King property, now a preserve, finally fell to ruins and was torn down.

Their land stretched along the line, and where others saw trees and shale, the Kings saw coal. Silas King built a town from the roots up—storefronts, a schoolhouse, a post office, company housing. Fifty or sixty people lived there, maybe more. His kin, Doc King, ran a saloon and store out of his home.

The town bore their name: King's Station and King's Switch. And the railway made it thrive.

An outbuilding on the old King Property, now a preserve

Even now, if you follow the Moonville Rail Trail, the bones of the place still show. The timber tunnel that once made a train path through a hillside still stands. Weather-worn. Dark. Reeking of creosote. Empty.

Or not entirely.

Just a mile down the tracks from King's Station was another settlement—Waterloo, later called Mineral. It had its own mines, its own hardships. But something else bound these two places together.

Not just the railroad.

They shared their dead.

And those dead didn't rest quiet.

King's Station Ghost Story: The Ghost Cat

They say the dead don't walk the Moonville Rail Trail. They stalk.

They slither. They crawl. And, apparently… they purr.

I've hiked that trail for years. I've seen and heard things I couldn't explain. Still, nothing unsettled me more than the thing that started following me from King Hollow—something small, light-footed, and deceptively sweet.

A cat.

Or something that used to be.

The Meowing in the Brush

It started like any other stray encounter. I was hiking near the cut by the old King Hollow station when I heard it—that unmistakable feline wail. That miserable, long, dragging *meeeooowww* from deep in the brush. A cry too sad to ignore. It echoed like a plea across the rail bed.

I followed the sound.

Through bramble.

Through blood-hungry thorns.

Through the kind of underbrush that leaves scars that you don't brag about.

Each time, the cry moved just ahead—tugging me deeper, always just out of reach.

A glimpse here. A flicker of fur there. Then nothing.

And yet, on the path again, it would come padding up behind me, weaving through my legs like it wanted to trip me. Typical cat behavior. Pet me or perish. Then it vanished as if the air itself swallowed it up.

The Dog That Didn't Bark

Now, I should've known something was off when Harley didn't react.

Harley is my rescue mutt, trail companion, and certified cat-hater. I've seen her stiffen like a board at the faintest whiff of feline. She doesn't chase—oh no. Harley prefers psychological warfare. She'll lift one lip like a snide threat, show a single glint of canine ivory, and growl so low it sounds like the dirt's doing the talking.

If a cat even thinks about crossing our path, Harley knows.

But not this one.

When the ghost cat first started following us, Harley didn't growl. She didn't snarl. She didn't even notice. Her hackles stayed flat. Her nose stayed dry. Not once did she so much as twitch. It was like the thing wasn't even there.

Which, of course, it wasn't. Not exactly.

The Cat That Wasn't

Now, I believe in ghosts—but I like to rule out raccoons, possums, wind, and weird lighting before I start blaming the undead. So I kept trying to catch the cat. With hands. With food. With reason.

But I was always a step too slow.

Or it was a step too smart.

Then came the night I left my trail cam set up at Moonville Tunnel. I'd finished my hike and left it recording the mouth of the tunnel for about fifteen minutes while I packed up.

There were no cat calls that night. No brushing against my leg. No meows. No tripping me while I struggled to walk in the dark.

But when I got home and played the video... there it was. A meow.

Plain as daylight.

Crisp, clean, and close—like it came from just outside the frame.

And no cat to be seen.

The Theory

I've come to believe that the little beast is a remnant. A spectral leftover. Someone's long-dead pet still patrolling the tracks of a town long buried by time and trees.

Maybe it's still looking for its owner.

Perhaps it's playing.

Or maybe it just enjoys watching hikers trip over their own feet in a panic. I'm not sure if it's clumsiness… or the cat's idea of a joke. Mine do the same thing when they're hungry—throw themselves underfoot like furry landmines. Nearly killing me just to make a point.

Fair warning—try to pet it, and you'll just be stroking the breeze, looking ridiculous to anyone nearby. And if you try to step over it? Well, not everyone sees the ghost cat—so you'll look like you're high-stepping over a log that isn't there.

So, if you're walking the Moonville Rail Trail and hear a soft "meow" behind you—resist the urge to turn.

Don't call, "Here, kitty kitty."

Don't shake a snack bag.

And for the love of all things holy, don't try to pet it.

Because if you do… you just might end up with a ghost cat.

And while they don't use litter boxes… they might try to take you to the otherworld with them.

King's Station Ghost Story: Eight Foot Ghost of King Tunnel

The old rail line that ran between Ingham Station and Mineral City was more than a shortcut—it was a lifeline. Straight as a rifle barrel, it carved through the high hills and narrow valleys, and coal miners and their families used it day and night. It was faster than the wagon road and far more dangerous.

To reach the other side, travelers had to cross wooden trestles high above Hewett Fork's shallow waters.

Worse—they had to step inside the long black throat of King Tunnel, a timber-framed gauntlet with no alcoves and no mercy. If a train came while you were in it, there was nowhere to run but forward—and nowhere to hide at all.

Further along the line were deep rock cuts with sheer sides carved through ridges too steep to climb. In those narrow passes, if the whistle blew, you had only seconds to scramble up stone… or fall.

Many didn't make it.

They were crushed.

Split.

Torn.

The trains didn't stop. Not for bodies. Not for screams.

The Abandonment

For fifty years after the line was abandoned, the forest swallowed it whole. Briars grew thick enough to trap even light. Trees split the rails, and dirt crept over the old ties.

The path vanished, nearly lost to time.

But time, in these hills, doesn't forget.

And neither do the dead.

Things began to stir when the old trackbed was finally cleared for hikers. Not just deer or coyote. Not just wind. Something older. Something buried deep with the bones of the crushed.

It began with small things.

EMF detectors going haywire.

Faint fiddle music where no house stood.

Laughter in places long empty.

Whispers in the middle of the day.

Then came the sightings.

Apparitions walked where cabins once leaned. Cameras caught full-bodied figures on fogless nights. And those who dared to hike the trail after dark—during ghost hunts and storytelling walks—felt the old presence return.

One spirit, though, stood apart from the rest.

And it didn't just appear.

It chased.

The Crawling Ghost of King Tunnel

He's been seen near King Tunnel.

Near Mineral City.

On the path toward Ingham Station.

Always at night. Never under a moon.

Witnesses describe a man—tall as two men, with brown skin and limbs too long for anything living. He walks like he's on stilts, but worse than walking, he crawls—arms bowed, legs bent backward, skittering over the ties with fingers that grip like claws.

And he wears a miner's cap.

The old kind.

With a flame that still burns, trailing down his back like it's burning his memory into the dirt he walks on.

They say he comes from the tunnel, hunched and waiting in the dark. And when he sees you, he starts to follow—not fast at first, but steady. As if the trail itself is unfinished, and your footsteps are leading him home.

The Man He Was

His name was Pleasant Dexter. Folks called him "Dex."

He was 23. A section man for the railroad. Worked the mines in Mineral City and lived with his parents in Ingham Station, just two miles up the line.

He was young. Restless. Walked barefoot sometimes because his boots hurt too much after a shift.

On the night of May 4, 1927, Pleasant left Mineral late as the young and wild at heart do. He said goodnight to friends, complained of aching feet, took off his boots, and started walking home. He trudged barefoot over splintered ties, maybe a bit late-winter and early-spring melancholy holding on to him, tired, done.

He never made it.

Somewhere near King Tunnel, Pleasant lay down on the rails and fell asleep. Three trains passed through that night. No one knows which one tore him apart. A man found what was left the next morning—his body broken and bent, his feet bloodied and worn. One eye was still open as if he hadn't quite seen it coming.

Still Walking

It wasn't long before the stories started.

A figure seen on the tracks just past the tunnel. A man limping, then crawling. A glint of flame moving low to the ground like a candle dragged through the mud.

He always heads toward Ingham Station.

Always along the rails.

Always crawling like the bones in his body don't fit anymore.

Some think he doesn't know he's dead.

Others say he does—and he's angry no one stopped the train.

A few believe he's still trying to get home. The house is long gone now, but he doesn't know that either.

He's seen most often by those walking alone.

And if you ever cross King Tunnel after dark, don't stop to listen.

Don't turn around if you hear something creeping just behind you on the wooden ties.

Because if it's Pleasant Dexter...he doesn't walk anymore.

He crawls.

And he's faster than he looks.

The Town: Mineral City

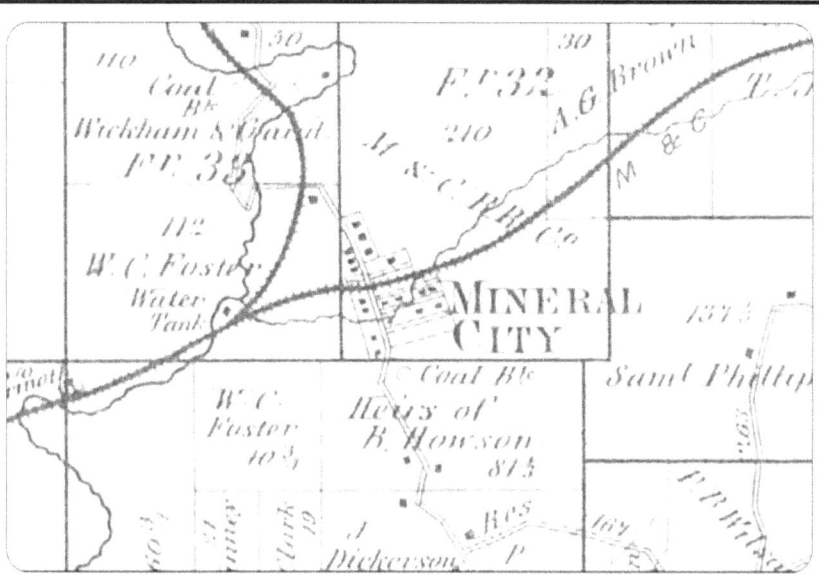

Mineral City: A Stop on the Line

Along Hewitt Fork, Mineral (once known as Mineral City or Waterloo) emerged as a coal port along the old Marietta & Cincinnati Railroad in Athens County.

Established in the late 1850s, it was built atop seams of coal and centered around a bustling post office—reportedly the smallest in Ohio until its closure in 1966.

Mineral served as a vital link between Athens County's rural settlements and the wider world. Here, the placid waters of Mud Lick Run ran into Hewitt Fork, carrying refuse-stained waters from distant pits and echoing with the sound of loaded coal cars rolling by.

In its heyday:

Miners and their families lived in tight-knit company houses.

A one-room school and general store served daily needs.

The air smelled of steam, coal dust, and the distant whistle of the B&O trains.

By the early 1900s, coal seams began to dry up, and trains slowed. The post office shuttered in the 1960s, and the tracks that once carried ore and passengers were dismantled in the 1980s.

But the town never entirely disappeared. Some historic houses remain scattered along Route 356. The old rail bed has been reborn as part of the Moonville Rail Trail, linking Zaleski, Moonville, Ingham, King's Station, and Mineral along a path now traveled by hikers and ghost-hunters alike.

Today, Mineral lies nearly silent—but not empty. Echoes linger of midnight whistles, clattering coal cars, and footsteps through the tunnel. The forest has reclaimed much, but memory endures.

Mineral City Ghost Story: It Ain't No Whistlin' Jack

In the early 1900s, Ernest Keeton started working in the Moonville area mines at a young age. When shifts ran late, he would walk the railroad home in the dark.

One night, between Mineral and Ingham Station, Ernest heard a sound in the trees.

Phweet. Phweet.

Click. Click. Click.

In the Appalachian hills and hollers, those sounds meant only one thing: Whistlin' Jack.

The Sound in the Trees

Old folks claimed Whistlin' Jack was something between beast and devil—a creature shaped like a cougar, whistling and clicking its claws with a high-pitched sound, like a metal fork tapping and dragging across a plate.

It lured travelers with a soft whistle, then struck just after the clicking began.

Phweet. Phweet.

Click. Click. Click.

Those who followed the sound never came back. The whistle pulled you in; the click came before the end.

Ernest quickened his pace. The whistle came again—closer.

Phweet. Phweet.

Click. Click. Click.

He turned and saw it: a white shape drifting behind him, gliding above the rails. Too smooth to be human.

Phweet. Phweet. Click. Click. Click.

Phweet. Phweet. Click. Click. Click.

Phweet. Phweet. Click. Click. Click—

Too solid for mist.

The faster he moved, the faster it came.

When he stopped, it hovered. Closer. Then the whistle broke—shrill, choking, like something breathing through blood.

Phweet. Phweet.

Click. Click. Click.

That's when he ran.

The Floating Cloth

Ernest sprinted for Moonville Tunnel. The thing kept pace with him, step for step—a fold of white, fluttering like a handkerchief in the wind. It pulsed with each whistle, each note a dying gasp.

Phweet. Phweet. Click. Click. Click.

Phweet. Phweet. Click. Click. Click.

Phweet. Phweet. Click. Click. Click—

Just as he reached the tunnel's mouth, the shape veered off into the trees. Silence fell. But Ernest knew he'd have to walk that way again come morning.

The Old Woman's Warning

That night, Ernest found himself in the company of an old woman and recounted what he'd seen.

"Phweet. Phweet. Click-click," he said, his hands trembling. "You got anything to keep it away?"

She rocked back and forth, her eyes narrowed in thought. "What kind of whistle was it?"

"Like something trying to get my attention, then a pop—like rotted bones cracking."

The old woman gave a dry chuckle. "Well, boy, I think I know what you're hearing. Want the good news or the bad news first?"

"Let's get the bad news over with."

She leaned in, her voice dropping. "Well, the bad news is that thing following you ain't no Whistlin' Jack."

A chill crept up Ernest's spine. What could possibly be the good news if it wasn't Whistlin' Jack?

After a long pause, she finally said, "When I was young, there was a girl named Sarah—a new bride, a new mother. She used to walk those same tracks, whispering to herself. One morning, they found her in the privy—her throat cut ear to ear with her own kitchen knife." The old woman took a long breath, then let it out with her lips pursed tightly, like a kiss. "They buried her in a white frock and tucked her handkerchief with her. Ever since, men have seen something white following them—a scrap of cloth drifting beside the track. The whistle? That's just her trying to breathe through the hole she made in her windpipe."

She gave a slow, knowing nod—the kind only women who'd lived a long time knew how to give. "Good news is, it ain't no demon—just a mean-spirited dead woman with her throat slit and a knack for crackin' her knuckles to get your attention. And Ernest, you're still young enough to outrun her!"

Here is how a couple of locals told the story—

Mrs. Forest Dearth

"I heard Ernest, One of the Keeton boys . . . heard him tell he was down in Moonville or maybe below there maybe, towards Mineral. . . in there somewhere. He was a'coming home in the night walking the railroad, of course people walked a lot then ya' know, and he said that there was someone who looked like he might have a sheet over him or something, ya' know, he couldn't tell and then he noticed it was running alongside of him, and Ernest said he started running and he'd run and this thing would run too and when he'd stop . . . it would stop, and he was scared to death! (much laughter) Finally it went on that way for a while and he said that all at once it just took of down over the bank and that was the last of him. I heard him tell that piece, now Ernest wouldn't lie about it . . . he was really scared. . . I don't know what it was . . . you speak of a ghost. I guess there are, I don't know." Mrs. Forest Dearth in interview by Rich Dahn.

Mr. Clyde Pinney

"There was a man by the name of Earnest Keeton that lived in the neighborhood. Earnest had the tendency to tip the bottle a little on occasion. Back at that time there was no road that led from Hope to Mineral. People walked the railroad back and forth, and he had been somewhere over in the vicinity of Mineral, possibly the church or whatever. But he was coming back by himself, and as he was walking along on one end of the ties he noticed on the opposite end of the ties there was a figure that was following right along beside of him at the same speed that he was traveling. He started to speed up a little bit and it speeded up a little bit and watched it and noticed that there was no sounds being made from the thing that was on the other end of the ties. And, the faster he went the faster it went, and he decided that he was gonna run of and leave it, so he ran and it ran the same speed that he ran. And it stayed with him until he got to the east end of the Moonville Tunnel, and when he started to go into the tunnel, it went down over the hill, away from the tunnel, it didn't come into the tunnel with him." - Interview with Clyde Pinney conducted by Kathy Simcox on February 23, 2003

Mineral City Ghost Story: Witches' Rock and the Devil's Tea Table

There's a place just past the Vinton County line in Athens County—off the Moonville trail and buried deep in the bluffs—where the trees thin, the wind turns strange, and the stone remembers.

They call it Witches' Rock. The legend starts not far from the Lawhead train wreck site, near Moonville, where the Moonville Ghost still drifts along the tracks.

But this is older than the wreck.

Older than the rails.

The Witches Met Here

They say witches met on that high stone outcrop—twelve at a time, always twelve—standing shoulder to shoulder, heads bowed, humming in low, guttural tones. The sound rose like steam and sank like rot. It moved through the woods like smoke—twisting, pulling, dragging the unwilling to their doom.

People heard it at night.

A low drone riding the wind.

Something that didn't belong.

And when they got too close, when curiosity or madness pushed them near, the witches took them.

They were snatched from the ground and lifted through the trees with the crack of branches and the sting of bloodied briars.

Whipped. Lashed.

Faces carved by thorns and claws.

But the worst came after.

The Devil's Tea Table

They were carried—still alive—to a second place. A weathered sandstone pillar near Mineral, where a flat rock teetered on top like it might fall if the wind so much as coughed.

They called it the Devil's Tea Table.

That's where he danced. Not a storybook devil with horns and hooves—a thing made of ash and heat, with coal-pit eyes and teeth like broken glass.

Don't Look Into the Devil's Eyes

He danced barefoot across the stone, twisting and leaping, skin smoking where it touched.

And if he stopped dancing long enough to look into your eyes—really look—he'd see straight through to your sins.

If your soul was clean, he'd vanish. You'd wake up days later, miles away, with thorn scars on your arms and no memory of how you got home.

But if you weren't clean…

He'd take it.

Your soul.

Gone like a spark in the wind.

And your body?

Dropped.

Over the edge of the table. Bones shattered. Mouth wide. Eyes still open.

Some say that's what the humming really is—not witches, but their victims, caught in a loop of endless falling. Still calling out as they hit the rock below.

And if you walk too close at dusk…you might hear them scream.

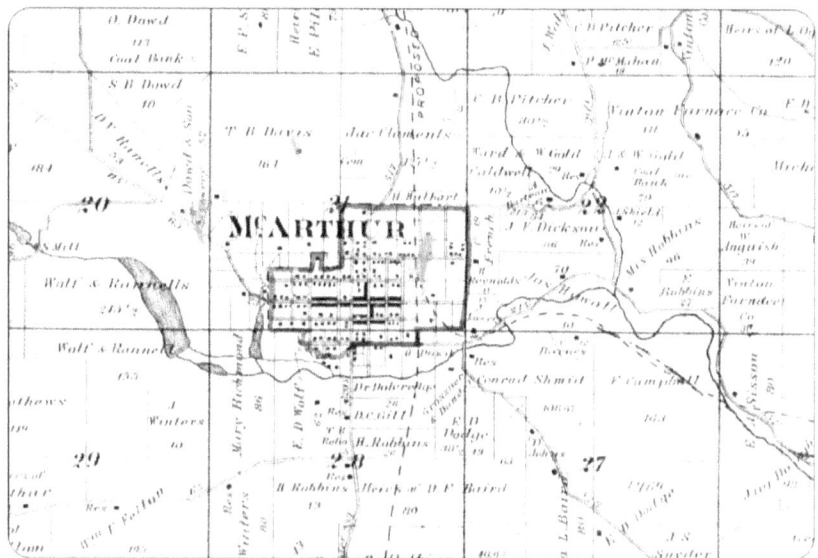

The Town: McArthur

Beyond the Tracks: The Ghosts of McArthur

Not all hauntings follow the railroad. Just a few miles south of Moonville, tucked deep in the heart of Vinton County, lies McArthur—the county seat and a town older than the rail itself.

While the Marietta & Cincinnati Railroad cut through the forests to the north, McArthur remained a vital hub—tied to those rail towns not by track but by blood.

Families stretched between the hills—brothers working the mines in Moonville, sisters married off near King Station, children sent back and forth along dirt roads and wagon ruts. Church picnics, funerals, and Saturday markets pulled folks from Hope Furnace Station and Ingham down into McArthur.

And when things went wrong—accidents, crimes, disappearances—it was often in McArthur where the stories were first whispered.

And while a different rail line thundered through town, a different breed of spirits also came with it—spreading fear like smoke in the hollows.

And some never left.

These are the ghosts that haunt the spaces between.

The ancient creeks.

The wooded lots.

The forgotten wells.

The places not marked on any map—but remembered all the same.

McArthur Ghost Story: Dead Peddler of Elk Fork

Before the Marietta and Cincinnati Railroad cut its way through the hills... before Moonville had its tunnel and Ingham its station... before maps gave names to specks of coal camps and cuttings...there was McArthur.

Not the town of today, but a rising quarry village— half-cleared, mud-tracked, and sharp with stone dust. The Musselman Rock Mill Quarries carved deep wounds into the earth along the Elk Fork.

And around them, the people came.

In the early 1800s, about fifty families scraped together a life here. They built cabins along the wagon road threading from Chillicothe through what would become McArthur and beyond toward Athens and its rough, waiting hills.

But something was wrong in the hollow.

The Screaming Creek

Travelers began whispering of screams that rose like steam shrieking from a teapot in the narrow cut just off the road—a voice that wasn't quite human.

Others spoke of a headless figure wandering near the quarries after dusk. At first, just glimpses.

Then encounters.

John Dillon, a shoemaker by trade, had heard the stories but thought little of them. Most men in McArthur did. Superstition couldn't mend soles or feed a family. Dillon worked long hours, and it wasn't unusual for customers to knock at his door after sundown.

One evening, a neighbor brought boots in need of stitching. Dillon, by candlelight, worked the thread through the worn leather, finishing the job with weary hands. He passed the boots to the man, exchanged a few words, and sent him on his way.

Minutes later, something thudded against his door. Then again—THUD. THUD. THUD.

Dillon opened the door.

The same neighbor stood there, trembling and wild-eyed, his lip bloodied from a fall on the porch steps.

His voice shook as he spoke. "A woman," he said, "tall as a pine… forty foot if she was a lick… ghost-white. She blocked the trail and wouldn't move. I tried to shove past her. My fists passed through."

The town buzzed with the story. But for some of the older folks, it wasn't a surprise.

They remembered the quarry ghost.

The Peddler's End

Years earlier, a traveling peddler passed often along the same trail that now bore screams and spirits. He was well-liked—a cheerful man with a heavy beard and a four-wheeled buggy filled with wares: delicate lace, silver spoons, ribbons, and sweet candy for children.

He made himself a regular fixture in the hollows, welcomed into homes, fed well, and sent on his way with coin and warm goodbyes.

Until one day… he vanished.

No one saw him again. Weeks passed. While tracking a deer along the shallow, meandering stream known as Elk Fork, a hunter discovered something unusual that did not belong.

There, by a great stump where a workman's ax had been forgotten, was a patch of blood-soaked brush. The ground was thrashed—trampled as if by many boots. A streak of something slick clung to a log.

Closer inspection revealed the truth:

A slice of human skin—still clinging with whiskers.

The same red-brown throat beard the peddler wore.

Theories spread fast.

"He didn't hear 'em coming," one man said.

"They brained him with the ax, quiet-like. Didn't dare fire a shot—would've given them away."

Sometime later, a traveler stumbled across the peddler's buggy—smashed and half-buried in a gulch, wheels askew like broken legs.

But his head was never found.

Not whole, anyway.

A Thing That Watches

After that, folks said the area around the Elk Fork was cursed. And as the town grew, so did the tales.

Some say the woman seen on the trail isn't a woman at all—but the echo of the peddler's final terror stretched into something massive and impossible. Others swear it is the peddler... still walking, headless, dragging his boots through pine needles and wet leaves, sniffing out the men who took what was his.

And when the wind curls along the Elk Fork after dark...

As it snakes past the edge of McArthur, slipping west toward Peacock Road and Locust Grove, or dips low along Route 50 like it's hunting the path to Prattsville—

It moves like something remembering.

Tracing the old streambed, the peddler once followed.

The same water that saw his boots.

And maybe...his blood.

When it howls through the trees like it's dragging something behind it...

You'd best stay on the lighted paths.

Even now, long after the quarry closed and the stones stopped screaming under the hammer, people coming home from late-night events at the high school take the long way. They avoid the area of Peacock Road.

They say the spirit doesn't just haunt.

It remembers.

And it waits.

Sometimes they see it.

Sometimes, it sees them.

But either way—someone always leaves the path.

And someone doesn't come back.

McArthur Ghost Story: The Ghost of Enos Kay

Long ago, off Route 50 leaving McArthur and heading toward Chillicothe, a stretch of dirt road curled through the dense woods over Salt Creek, and across that creek stood Timmons Covered Bridge.

This wooden corridor swallowed the light and silenced sound.

People spoke in hushed tones of what roamed there, of the ghost that gnashed its teeth at young lovers.

They said you could feel it in your chest before you saw it—something hateful breathing just inches from your skin.

One dark evening, a young couple in a horse-drawn buggy entered the bridge.

They kissed, briefly.

A moment later, the top of the buggy snapped down like the jaws of a trap, the boards splintering with a sickening crack.

The horse shrieked and bolted, but not before the man caught a glimpse above: a rotting face, smeared in shadow, drifting slowly down—eyes hollow, mouth twisted. The horse fled without them, leaving the couple bruised and bloodied in the dust. They never returned.

But they weren't the only ones. More than a few couples who dared to stop inside Timmons Bridge would walk home in silence, shaken and scratched, lips never again pressed together. Some claimed the bridge bled, black sap oozing from its beams, sticky and cold like a corpse's sweat. In time, lovers began to avoid the bridge entirely—as if something in them knew.

The ghost, they said, belonged to Enos Kay, a once-handsome farm boy from nearby Hamden.

He had eyes like sweet dusk and a heart full of Alvira—a girl who once promised him forever. He saved for two years to marry her, planning their secret meetings beneath the cover of the bridge's shadows.

But evil doesn't always wear horns.

At a church picnic days before the wedding, a stranger arrived: Mr. Brown. Charismatic. Tall. Predatory.

With a grin and a slice of apple pie, he stole everything from Enos.

In a single golden afternoon, Alvira fell under Brown's spell. Within two nights, she climbed down from her bedroom window and ran off into the dark, leaving Enos with nothing but a ring and a promise never kept.

The Curse

The whispers started almost immediately—neighbors buzzing over the elopement, Alvira's laughter echoing through the town while Enos stood in the shadows, fists clenched and soul unraveling. One night, mad with grief and rotting from the inside, he stood on the bridge, raised his voice to the sky, and screamed:

"I'll kill myself, and I'll curse this bridge! I'll haunt every fool lover 'til the end of time!"

He was found swinging two days later, his body contorted in a death-throe no man deserved, hung from the very rafters where Alvira had once kissed him.

The Haunting

Then the hauntings began.

Couples thrown from wagons. Horses screaming and refusing to cross. Glimpses of a long-limbed shadow crawling the beams above. Nails dragged across carriage tops. Cold breath on the back of the neck. And always—always—a scent of decayed apple pie. Eventually, the bridge was torn down and replaced by a newer road to handle the growing traffic from Chillicothe to Athens.

Today, only the whisper of Salt Creek remains, trickling over stones like the last heartbeat of a forgotten corpse.

But don't relax too soon.

They say Enos still lingers, especially on quiet nights when the moon is a sliver, and the trees lean in close. Park your car in a dark, remote spot near the old road, sneak a kiss, and listen.

If the air turns cold and heavy...

If your windows fog without reason...

If you hear something land on your roof with a snap...

Just know—you've caught the attention of Enos Kay,

and he's never forgiven lovers.

Not then.

Not now. Not ever.

McArthur Ghost Story: The Devil Went Down to Vinton County . . .

It was February of 1886. A biting wind howled across Vinton County, and in the small, weather-worn Macedonia Church, the flames of revival were burning hot. The people had gathered not for comfort but for warfare of the soul. They sang until their voices cracked. They prayed until their knees bruised. They believed the power of God would shake the very rafters.

And one night, it did.

The Devil Came Down to Vinton County

But not in the way they expected.

According to the Hocking Sentinel, during the height of the revival, as the congregation stood gathered around the altar, something walked in. Not from the back. Not from the side. But right up to the front.

"The Devil appeared in person before the altar... He was a giant in size and had hands with claws like an eagle, and head and horns like a Texas steer, and as black as coal. When spoke to, he would not answer or leave—until prayer was offered."

– Hocking Sentinel, Feb. 11, 1886

He didn't burst through the doors or come cloaked in fire. He simply materialized, massive and silent.

His skin was slick and coal-black.

Claws like knives hung from hands too long, twitching like they hungered for something.

His face—if you could call it that—was distorted, crowned with thick, twisted horns.

Eyes burned like cinders, locked on the altar.

The room dropped into a suffocating silence. But the people did not run.

They stood.

Mothers clutched children, not in panic but in protection.

Old men tightened calloused hands into fists.

The preacher, pale but firm, stepped forward and lifted his voice—not in fear, but in defiance.

They called down prayer like thunder.

Voices rose, scripture rang out. It was not pretty. It was not polite.

It was warfare—the kind of spiritual resistance that shakes unseen realms.

And slowly—painfully—the figure began to fade. Not like a ghost, but like something being forced out, pulled back into whatever pit it had crawled from. As it vanished, the heat in the room lifted, and the people stood in a silence heavy with holy awe.

It Left Empty-Handed

Something came to Macedonia once—dark, ancient, and full of malice.

And it left empty-handed.

He didn't steal a soul.

He didn't win the night.

And he never came back.

Because the people there didn't run.

They faced him. They held the line.

So if you ever think about bringing trouble to Vinton County...

Just remember—even the Devil didn't make it out with what he came for.

Local Cemeteries

Cemeteries used by the communities include:

Moonville, also known as Coe Cemetery (Moonville)

Township Hwy 18
McArthur, OH 45651
39.306453, -82.325125
(Graves: about 28 known)

Pioneer Cemetery (located at Hope Furnace off Olds Hollow Trail)

State Route 278
McArthur, Ohio 45651
39.32500, -82.34047
(Graves: more than 5 known)

Hewett Cemetery (Mineral)

Grass Run Road
(Township Road 262)
Mineral, Ohio 45766
39.34890, -82.24530
(Graves: about 28 known)

Keeton Cemetery (Zaleski)

Park Road 9
Zaleski, Ohio 45698
39.32330, -82.35970
(Graves: about 155
known)

Saint Sylvester Catholic Cemetery (Zaleski)

Jamison Road
Zaleski, Ohio, 45698
39.28360, -82.40610
(Graves: over 590 known,
still in use)

Ferguson Cemetery (New Marshfield)

Robinette Ridge Road
(County Road 255)
New Marshfield, Ohio
45766
39.30330, -82.29750
(Graves: about 8 known)

What the Tracks Remember— Deaths Along the Railway

The ghosts of Theodore Lawhead, the Lavender Lady, the Bully, and the Drunk Brakeman are the ones most often spoken of—the names passed down, the dead remembered. But those who walk the old rails have told me of others. Strangers. Shadows. Figures that appear in the dark and disappear just as fast, leaving behind only a chill and the feeling that they're still waiting.

Waiting to be known. Waiting to be heard.

We may never know who they were. The ground around Moonville and the tracks that cut through it claimed at least twenty-six lives—crushed, mangled, lost to fire and misstep. And not all their names were kept.

Some ghosts never tell you who they are.

They just follow. They just watch.

These are a few whose stories may one day rise—or already have arisen and how they met their end:

Jumping a Train

February 1876—13 year old Henry Shirkey

The McArthur Enquirer, of last week, says: As we go to press this (Thursday) afternoon we learn that Henry Shirkey, the youngest son of John Shirkey, of Vinton Station, was severely injured by jumping from a box car of a freight train going West about one-fourth of a mile west of Vinton Station, at a quarter past 4 o'clock on Wednesday evening, and died 20 minutes before 6 o'clock this (Thursday) morning.
Athens Messenger, Feb 17, 1876

May 1880—30 year-old James Hood

James Hood, aged about thirty, a resident of Zaleski, while returning from Athens on the fast line on Friday, attempted to jump off the train one quarter mile east of the depot, and opposite his home. In doing so he was thrown about twenty feet against a post, and his neck broken. He has been in the habit of jumping off trains at this point in order to save walking back from the depot. He leaves a wife and three children.

Athens Messenger, May 20, 1880

September 1907—Allen Albaugh

Luhrig, O., Sept. 4.—The badly mangled body of Allen Albaugh, a middle aged miner of this place, was found under some underbrush near Moonville Saturday. Albaugh, accompanied by his brother got on a passing train and started for Zaleski. It is supposed that he staid on the train until a tunnel was reached, and that he was knocked off in some manner. When the body was found, one hand was cut off. Search was made for the missing man but not until a week later was the body found.

Athens Messenger & Herald Sept 1907

Brakemen Falling Under Wheels

March 1859—Unknown Brakeman

Brakeman on the Marietta and Cincinnati Railroad fell from the cars and was fatally injured. Due to "too free use of liquor."

McArthur Democrat, March 31, 1859

July 14, 1873—McDevitt

Conductor Gallagher's Accommodation, on the M. & C. road east Monday morning at about half-past 6 o'clock when nearing Moonville Station collided with a freight train. A brakeman of the accommodation named McDevitt was caught between two colliding platforms and had both legs and one arm horribly mangled. McDevitt survived his injuries but a short time. No one else on either train was hurt.—The deceased we learn was about 21 years of age and leaves a widowed mother. (Occurred one half mile east of Moonville.) Athens Messenger, July 17, 1873

1874 / 1884—Thomas & Michael Malborough

Michael Molboro is killed on the Marietta and Cincinnati Line. Eight years later his brother, Thomas, a brakeman is killed on the same track.
The Vinton Record, 14 Feb 1884

Walking in Front/Behind of Train

June 1859—Joshua Sands

Railroad Accident-Death of a Good Citizens. Mr. Joshua Sands, an estimable citizen of this County, and agent at Big Sand Switch, was run over by the locomotive tender on Monday last, and almost instantly killed. It appears that a locomotive was backing up to the station at the Big Sand Switch, when Mr. S. stepped upon the track, for the purpose of taking the number of a car loaded with iron ore, it is supposed, and did not notice the almost noiseless approach of the locomotive. . . McArthur Democrat June 30, 1859

February 1871—John Thomas
John Thomas, an employee of Hope Furnace Co, was killed on the Hope Furnace R.R. on the 13th. He was driving a team which was hauling a car loaded with pig iron, when he slipped and fell on the track, the front wheel of the car passing over his body, killing him instantly. Mr. T. was about sixty years old, a sober, industrious man, a member of the M.E. church and leaves a large family—
The Vinton record. February 02, 1871

January 1893—John Lawhead
Laid to Rest. The burial of Mr. John Lawhead, whose death resulted from the injuries he received by being run over by the cars at Mineral City last Friday morning, took place in this city yesterday afternoon-the interment was made in the station graveyard.
Chillicothe Gazette January 9, 1893 Page 1

May 1936—Amzy Kennard
Vinton Man Is Killed by Train Amzy Kennard Dies Instantly When Struck at Moonville Crossing Sunday NEW MARSHFIELD Amzy E Kennard, age 72, was instantly killed when struck by Baltimore and Ohio Train No, 3, at the Moonville Crossing near his home in Vinton County at 11:00 a.m. Sunday—Athens Messenger May 11, 1936

Fall from Bridges

January 1857—Unknown Man

Another Sad Catastrophe. We learn that a man returning from a grocery near Moonville, in this county to his home, fell from a railroad bridge which he, attempted to cross and was instantly killed. The report of the catastrophe was soon spread, and the people, incensed at the grocery keeper, collected, broke into his establishment and destroyed a considerable quantity of the "ardent." He has resorted to the law for redress of grievances and the case will probably come before the Probate Court at its next session. We did not learn the name of the deceased. McArthur Democrat., Jan 15, 1857

July 1978—Wendy Fairchild

A 13-year-old Columbus girl died in a fall from a railroad trestle Saturday in Vinton County near Zaleski. Wendy Fairchild was on a hiking trip with a minister and three other children when she fell from a trestle of the Moonville tunnel of the C&O Railroad. A spokesman from the Vinton County Sheriff's Department said the girl fell while a train was passing over the trestle at 5:46 p.m. The accident is still under investigation by the department. Chillicothe Gazette July 10, 1978

Suicides

June 27, 1855—James McGrath

Found Dead On the morning of the 27th of June, an Irishman by the name of James McGrath, aged 27 years, was found dead, hanging upon a tree near the house of Mr. Ferguson, Brown township, Vinton County, Ohio. McArthur Democrat., July 06, 1855

1868—Nathan Brewer

A 58 year-old fights a court battle with a local bully and takes his life—Mister Nathan Brewer, an old and well-known citizen of our county, committed suicide near Sand Station—About two months since he made complaint against David Keeton, one of his neighbors—Vinton Record March 4, 1868

June 1878—Sarah Hewitt

The wife [Sarah] of Lafayette Hewitt, living about two miles from Mineral City, this county, and who has been married about a year, made a desperate attempt on Saturday to destroy herself by cutting her throat with a razor, completely severing the windpipe and causing injuries that in the opinion of one of her attending physicians, whom we have seen, that will probably result fatally. Mrs. H. who had an infant a few weeks ago—Athens Messenger June 9, 1878

Walking the Tracks

August (18) 1873—Elizabeth Bryson Brewer (age 37)

Mrs. Brewer, wife of Thomas Brewer, and a daughter of Abram Bryson, living at Zaleski, in this county, came to her death on Monday evening last, by being struck on the head by the Cincinnati Express Train, bound east, about 2 o'clock. She was walking upon the track about one and a half miles east from that place, and on the approach of the train she stepped off the track, but, in making an effort to reach the track again, not observing that the train was out of reach, she stepped so close that some part of the rear car struck her on the head, crushing the skull, and causing death about four hours afterward. Democratic Enquirer Aug 20, 1873 Page 3

October 1873—Unknown woman

While we delayed for a few minutes at Moonville on last Monday we heard reference to the instant killing of a woman in the deep cut near that town the day previous by the morning express. The name of the woman we failed to ascertain. Athens Messenger October 16, 1873

April 13, 1879—Bartolomeu "Bancrats" Betz

Bummgrattus Betts, man aged German residing at Hope Furnace, four miles east of here, was instantly killed this afternoon by the east bound freight while walking on the tracks. The Stark County Democrat, April 17, 1879.jpg

January 1890—Mary Shea

Friday, January 10, 1890 - Mrs. Mary Shea, of Moonville, aged 80, fatally hurt by a train. Mrs. Patrick Shea (in her eighties and a grandmother of Michael Shea) was walking the Moonville to Hope and while crossing the trestle was struck by a train. Her leg had to be amputated and she died from the shock. Steubenville Weekly Herald, January 10, 1890

November 1892—76 year-old Deborah Allen

The funeral train over the Baltimore and Ohio Railroad conveying to Little Hocking for burial the remains of William Chambers, who was killed in the wreck at Roxabel, struck an old woman named Deborah Allen at Moonville and she was instantly killed. So fast was the train running that before it could be brought to a stand the body of the poor woman was carried a distance of 100 yards and pitched over a trestle thirty feet high. Delphos Weekly Herald, Nov 17 1892

June 1902—Charles Ferguson

The west bound B & O. S.-W. morning freight through here on Sunday morning killed an old man at Moonville, Athens county. The train broke at Moonville and the old man, whose name as not been learned here, attempted to cross between the sections, resulting in his death.
Chillicothe Gazette June 16, 1902

February 1929—Erastus Dexter

In February of 1929, when he was 61 while working in a coal mine in McConnelsville, Pennsylvania, he died in a mining accident. They brought him home and buried him in the New Marshfield Cemetery, about seven miles from Moonville.

Working on Bridge/Trestles

October 1945—George Gilpin

Injured Saturday morning in an accident on a bridge construction job at Moonville, died. . . The victim was struck by a load of ties he was lifting, and was pinned against the-side of a flat car. Athens Messenger Oct 15, 1945

Falling asleep on the tracks

1874—Levi Sales (about age 24)

Levi Sales of Moonville was run over and killed by the Fast Stock last Sunday morning. He had been at Zaleski and it was supposed he had got under the influence of liquor, laid down upon the track and gone to sleep.
Vinton Record., June 04, 1874

Train wrecks

1880—Engineer Theodore Lawhead

Frank [Theodore] Lawhead, Engineer Killed in Train Wreck Near King's station in this county on Thursday last. Engineer Lawhead and Charles Krick, fireman, both of Chillicothe, were instantly killed by collision of freight trains, which, we are told, was the result of a mistake of train dispatcher. The trains were totally wrecked. . .

Athens Messenger, Thursday November 11, 1880

1938—Charles Landrum, age 54

1938 Charles Landrum, Engineer Killed in Train Wreck—A heavily loaded Baltimore & Ohio Railway double-header freight train crashed into a fall of rock at 11:57 p.m. Monday night killing the engineer on one of its two engines. The mishap occurred six miles east of Zaleski between Hope and Moonville. . . The Portsmouth Times, December 27, 1938

1874—Unknown Fireman

There was a smash-up of two freight trains at Moonville, on Tuesday, by which eleven cars were wrecked and a fireman killed, whose name we did not learn.

Vinton Record., July 16, 1874

Murder and Accidental Deaths

1867—Murder of Scott Brothers

Our readers will perhaps remember of the destruction by fire of a cabin, belonging to Hope Furnace Co., near Zaleski, some five years since, and that its two occupants, young men named Scott, were, it was reported and believed, burned to death in it. Later information leads to the conclusion that they were murdered...John Slavens, who was working at Hope Furnace at the time of the fire went from there to Tennessee, where, lately, he murdered his nephew, for which he was tried, found guilty, and sentenced to the Penitentiary for a long term of years. Before, however, he was forwarded to the Penitentiary ...he or his wife confessed to the murder of the two Scott boys and that he had fired the cabin to hide the deed, which was done for money. The citizens of the neighborhood in which Slavens was imprisoned became exasperated on learning of this double crime, broke open the prison and hanged him.
The Vinton Record McArthur, Ohio July 25, 1872 Page 3

April 1876—30 year-old Catherine Moriarty

A woman named Moriarty met with a horrible death by burning, on Saturday, near Rew Station on the M. & C. road, a short distance from Moonville [Area just after 2nd trestle beyond tunnel]. While engaged at burning brush she was taken with an apoplectic fit and falling backward in the fire was almost wholly consumed before her situation was discovered.
Athens Messenger April 13, 1876

January 1877—Edmund Dunn

At Hope Furnace Station, January 18, 1877 Grocer Edmund Dunn was stabbed and killed by 14 year old Michael Clifford over the purchase of alcohol.

July 1890—Ella Friend
Only last week a young girl named Ella Friend on her way
home near Hope Furnace, was waylaid by three brutes
named Ed Dunn, Marion Bell, and Shive Collins, who
outraged her and then choked and beat and bruised her in
such a manner that she has since died from her injuries—
The Hocking Sentinel July 30, 1890

May 1899—Cliff Coe
Coe (one of the family members of the original landowners)
died of a heart attack inside the depot in May 1899 while
holding a child (Ruthie).

A four-year-old child, Albert Stillwell, died in 1900 by choking
on a .22 gun cartridge.

Bessie Stillwell, died from a cup of coffee being dropped on
her back in 1910.

February 1921—Raymond Burritt
Herbert Raymond Burritt February 3, 1921, age 17, coal
miner died in a mining accident at the Moonville mine.

December 1923—Timothy Clifford,
December 2, 1923 Timothy Clifford 40, recluse living near
Hope, was found dead in his home yesterday, having been
killed by the discharge of a falling shotgun. "Timothy
Clifford, who accidentally shot and killed himself on
December 2. Mr. Clifford was a farmer living near Athens
and was examining a revolver before several friends when
the gun was accidentally discharged, the bullet entering the
chest near the heart."
The Times Recorder Zanesville, Ohio Dec 6, 1923 Page 1

Moonville Ghostly Images

Photo courtesy: Michelle Schrader.

The original photo as submitted by Michelle Schrader. Here is her story: "I was camping at Lake Hope and I fully intended on visiting the Moonville Tunnel while I was there. I had previously visited the tunnel before this particular visit. I went with two other friends in the middle of the day last fall, at the beginning of October. We took a bunch of pictures, I was using my digital camera. I did not notice that there was a figure in the picture until I downloaded it on to my computer when I got home. Upon magnifying the shadow, it appears to be a manly looking figure. It gave me complete chills. I have shared the picture with lots of people, and we are all baffled. There is no reasonable explanation for the figure. It does go along with the legend of the tunnel, though. Apparently, based on the story that I have heard, there was a brakeman that was killed in the tunnel, and if you look at the figure, it appears that his leg is missing from the photo, you can see right through his leg. Creepy, huh?"

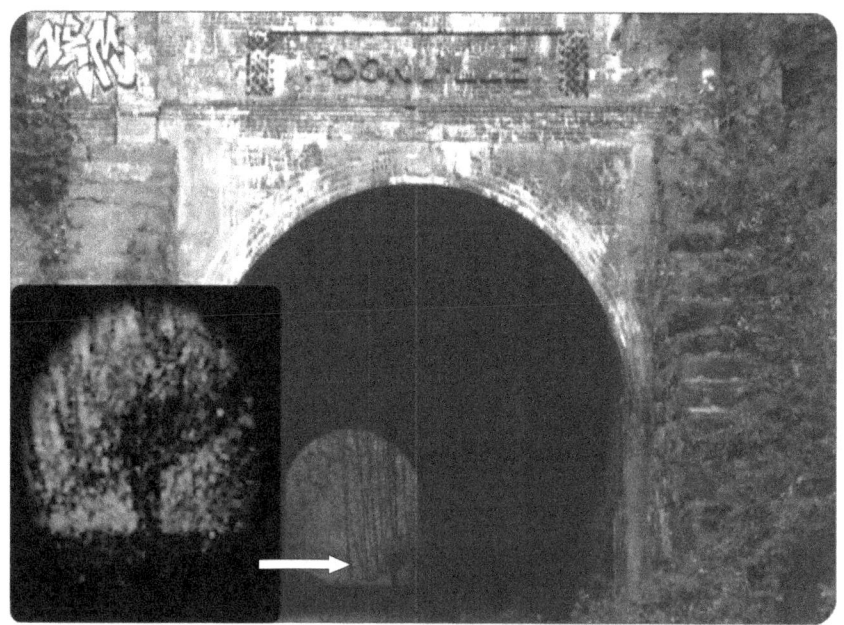

Photo courtesy: Nicholas Viltrakis.

About the Photo: A group of friends of mine (and I) were camping near lake hope 9/15/7 - 9/16/7 and we wanted to go on the haunted tour. It took us about two hours to find the train tunnel because we aren't the brightest or most organized, anyway. I am a professional photographer and I shot the whole weekend for fun. When we finally got to the easily found tunnel, I ran ahead to get a couple of shots of the spooky tunnel without people. I clicked off about 10 and then my group started filtering past me yelling through the tunnel. We ran all through the place and had a great time, I climbed it and posed on top and all. Nothing even remotely spooky or ghostly, nothing. Then when I was looking through the photos Sunday I was looking at them large and I noticed in this picture that there was the REAL figure of a person! We ran all through that tunnel and there was no one else there unless they were hiding in the woods until we left. Could be a shadow or tree or something, we really weren't checking around, we were mostly trying to scare each other and take pictures. I did lighten the lower corner of the end of the tunnel after I saw the figure so you could see it better— Nicholas Viltrakis

Jannette Quackenbush photo

About the Photo: This is my ghostly photo. It must have been around 2004 that I was visiting Moonville Tunnel with my family. It was a time when few people went out there barring locals fishing and swimming. We barely made it there because the Hope-Moonville Road was flooded and there were no cars and not another soul around. We had walked through the tunnel, hiked back into the forest, and trekked up above the tunnel to get a birds-eye view. At the time, the trestle/bridge by the parking lot was not there and we had to hike a trail in the bottomlands or wade the swollen creek. We chose to hike the trail. I had just gotten a video camera and started filming my daughter singing. We hung around a long time and there was absolutely no one else there. We went home and I pulled up the video and was startled to see a ghostly figure showing up at the far end of the tunnel. We did not see it with the naked eye.

Stories Along The Trail: The Goat Man

Something Walks the Trail

There's something strange on the trail. Not a ghost. Not a man. Not exactly an animal, either.

People don't like to talk about it outright, but I've heard the same story whispered three times now—from three different people. They didn't know each other. They told it years apart.

But the details line up.

Each time, it happened on a quiet stretch of the Moonville Rail Trail.

No one else around.

Just the sound of feet on gravel and birds going quiet in the trees.

And then...a feeling.

Like something was watching.

Like something wasn't right.

They all said it walked upright. They all said it had hooves. And not one of them ever went back to that part of the trail again.

The Goat Man Story . . .as told to me—

"I live in Gallia County, and the story about Moonville was passed on to me. Everybody used to talk about it [Goat Man] at school. It was about a Goat Man who walks the trail and hides in the woods. I didn't believe it. Then, one night, my friends and I drove up to Moonville and parked our car. We saw this big shadow come out when we got out and started across the steel bridge. We all started to run, but before we did, I could make out a creature that was part goat and part man. It had goat legs and hooves, and it started walking toward us. We screamed and ran all the way back to our car. I won't go back there. I know what I saw, and it was real. Other people have seen it, too."

Stories Along The Trail: The Ghost Train

The Train That Doesn't Know It's Dead

I've heard it more than once—a train where no train should be. A horn that blasts through the trees like a war cry. The shriek of steel on steel. The thunder of something huge and fast tearing through the dark.

But the rails are long gone. And still... it comes.

I've felt it—twice. A burst of wind so strong it nearly knocked me off the trail.

The sudden tremble of gravel underfoot.

The sense that if I didn't move, I'd be crushed beneath something I couldn't see.

I'm Not Alone

And I'm not the only one. Others have heard it.

Some swear they've seen the glow of a headlamp where there is no engine. Some say the trees bend away from the trail when it comes.

But here's the worst part—It doesn't slow down. It doesn't whistle for crossings. It doesn't seem to see you at all. Like it's still running a route, it doesn't realize it no longer exists. Like it doesn't know it's dead.

And if you're standing on the trail when it comes barreling through—you'd better pray it disappears before it gets to you.

Because whatever's driving that engine...is not watching the tracks.

The Ghost Train Story . . .as told to me—

"When I was walking down the trail before the bridges got in, my friends and I heard the sound of a train along the tracks. It was real. I mean, it was like a train was coming down those tracks, but the tracks aren't even there anymore. It had the sound of the horn and the wheels grinding the track, and it was so loud it sounded like it was going to hit us. We were so scared we really thought a train was coming through. We started to run and when it was almost right behind us, it just disappeared and was deathly quiet. No birds. No crickets. Nothing. My friend was crying and laughing at the same time."

My Weird Stories Along The Trail: Playing Hide and Seek With the Dead

Throughout the year, I lead night hikes and paranormal investigations in haunted wild areas, including Moonville along the old rail trail. Folks come for ghost stories and end up learning about everything from the local owls to the dead who never quite left. Coyotes howl, deer groan, owls scream, and sometimes something whistles that doesn't sound quite... feathered.

Most of it can be chalked up to nature.

But not all of it. Because most leave convinced they've met both.

Let me be clear: I've never been bitten, punched, scratched, or shoved. I don't feel anything evil out there. What I run into is something else entirely—ghosts, sure, but just... people. Dead people. Some nice, some cranky, some caught in tragedy. And a few who never got the memo that practical jokes are supposed to end with life.

Case in point:

One weekend, I had a group in their twenties—real ghost-hunting types, loaded with gear, gadgets, and enthusiasm. They were using a spirit box (basically a ghost walkie-talkie), and suddenly, a child's voice came through.

Somebody (probably the one with the headlamp on upside-down) chirped, "Wanna play hide and seek?"

And off they went—wandering the woods, pretending to find the ghost kid behind trees and bushes, giggling like it was a haunted playground.

Fun night. Everyone left happy.

What no one thought to ask was: *who else might be listening?*

The next weekend, I was heading out solo after a late investigation. It was darker than the inside of a coffin at Moonville. I was passing the old Coe homestead site when I saw it there by a tree, standing a tall, skinny figure with a real mop of hair.

Watching.

Now, I've hiked ghostly places enough to know better than to panic. So, I tried the polite route first.

"Well, hello," I said, my voice cracking like bad kindling. Then I chuckled nervously, trying to lighten the mood, "You startled me, friend. And that's not wise at my age—I'm liable to either pee myself, drop dead, or start shooting at shadows. And I didn't do the first or the last, so... let's not test the odds tonight."

Poof. Gone. Just vanished.

I blinked. Swallowed. Told myself it was some teen playing around. Naturally, I picked up the pace. Fast-walked like a suburban mall grandma. Then—at the next bend—I heard it. A faint, sing-song voice: "Over here!"

And there, at the next old homesite, another shadow. Leaning. Waving.

Poof. Gone again.

Now, I had a good twenty-minute walk left past the third abandoned homesite before I reached my Jeep. And I spent every one of those minutes thinking: They're playing hide and seek. With me.

DEAD PEOPLE are playing a game with me.

And let me tell you, nothing makes a hike feel longer than being the only living player in a ghostly contest.

It hasn't happened again. And I can't say I'm eager for a rematch. I like ghosts—I really do. But I prefer them not giggling in the dark, watching me try not to trip over my own fear while they count down:

"Ready or not, here we come!" Because I'm not sure what they would do if they caught me.

My Weird Stories Along The Trail: Knock Knock from the Beyond

People always ask me: "What's the scariest place you've ever been?" Or, "Which haunted spot messed you up the most?" And listen—I get it. I've visited over 3,000 haunted places. Not to brag (okay, maybe just a little), but it's part of the job.

I travel, I investigate, and I write the ghost stories that keep people up at night.

You'd think with that kind of resume, I'd have a solid "ghost tackled me down a hallway" story by now. But here's the truth:

More than a few places? Nothing out of the ordinary.

Sometimes, it's just creaky floorboards, a flying squirrel in the attic, or someone's overly enthusiastic uncle in a moth-eaten Civil War coat trying to look spooky. It doesn't mean the place isn't haunted—just that on that visit, the ghosts weren't taking appointments.

It's not that I don't believe. I do. But hauntings are rarely on-demand. You can't just strut into a graveyard and yell, "Ghost me, bro!" You've got to earn it—go again and again, build a rapport with the dead, like you're awkwardly dating a poltergeist.

And yes, people get mad when I don't pick their haunted barn as the most terrifying place on Earth.

I Have Weird Things Happen to Me

That said... I do have moments. Weird moments.

Some of the weirdest things happen at Moonville Tunnel, mostly because I'm there so often; the ghosts are starting to recognize me.

One of my go-to tools is the spirit box—basically a modified digital radio that rapidly scans through AM and FM frequencies. What you hear is a chaotic mix of white noise, static, fragments of music, DJ banter, commercials, and the occasional late-night rant.

Imagine a blender chewing through a talk show— that's the soundtrack.

But here's the theory: some believe that spirits can manipulate the snippets of sound or use the energy from the radio waves themselves to form actual responses. It's like giving a ghost access to a scrambled intercom. When using it, you listen closely for intentional words or phrases—something that stands out from the audio soup. And while it can spit out random chatter that means nothing, ask the right questions, and sometimes...you get answers that feel chillingly personal.

Knock Knock

To test it, I use a little trick: I ask it to say "Hello, Jannette." That way, if the box says my name, it's not just some random Top 40 mumble. It's intentional.

Now, for added flair (and because ghost hunting should be fun, right?), I've also been known to drop a knock-knock joke into the spirit box session. Yeah. I get it. It's dumb. I'll say, "Knock knock," and hope something answers "Who's there?" Then I throw out a name like Hatch, wait for "Hatch who?" and of course, I deliver the zinger:

"Bless you."

Cue ghostly eye-rolls. I've literally had the box groan back: "She's not funny."

Thank you, dearly departed critic.

Anyway, on this particular night, I ran through a few knock-knock routines at Moonville with nothing more than the occasional hiss and static sass. I moved on, asked some serious questions, packed up, and drove home in the fog like any normal ghost-hunting night.

Then I Went to Bed. That's When IT Happened.

Got home. I brushed my teeth. Crawled into bed.

Yawned.

And that's when it happened.

From the darkness at the foot of my bed, clear as if someone was standing there with their arms crossed and a smirk on their face, I heard:

"Knock. Knock."

Now, look—I do not believe in ghosts following people home.

This had never happened to me before.

But I also believe in survival.

So I did what any seasoned ghost hunter would do...I froze like a possum, wiggled deeper under the covers, and laid there for two hours, eyes wide open, heart racing, waiting for the punchline.

Spoiler: There wasn't one—just silence.

It never happened again. But I can promise you, in that moment, I was one bad knock-knock joke away from becoming a ghost myself.

Paranormal Investigations: What to Expect along the Rail Trail

People often arrive at a paranormal investigation not quite sure what to expect. Some imagine full-body apparitions or things flying across the room. Others think it's all just creepy campfire stories. The truth? It's somewhere in between—and that's where it gets exciting.

When I take groups on night hikes and paranormal investigations, we approach things with a blend of curiosity, folklore, and, yes—science. Paranormal researchers work under the theory that energy surrounds us and that spirits if they're out there, may be able to manipulate this energy to make contact.

To test that idea, we bring along some specialized tools. One of the most popular (and easy to use) is the  EMF detector—a device with a row of lights ranging from green to red. It measures big or small fluctuations in electromagnetic fields, which are invisible but naturally produced by things like electronics. So, when you're out on a remote trail, far from anything that should be setting it off... and it suddenly jumps to red? That's when the questions start.

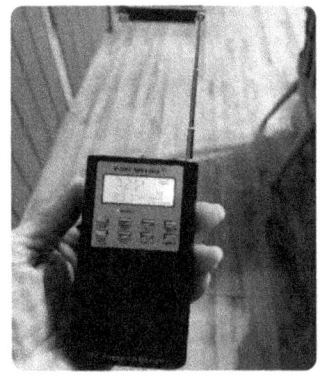

Another favorite tool is the spirit box—a modified digital radio that rapidly scans through AM or FM channels, creating a blend of white noise and fragments of voices or music.

Many believe that spirits can manipulate these sounds or use the radio waves to communicate. During a session, we listen closely for clear words or responses to specific questions. When it works, it can feel like you're eavesdropping—or even chatting a bit—with someone on the other side.

We also use video recorders, infrared, and full-

spectrum cameras—tools that can capture light and movement outside the range of human sight. I'll often catch things during review—shadows flitting across the frame, voices whispering back answers to questions we asked hours earlier—things we never noticed in the moment.

But here's something important to remember, especially along the Moonville Rail Trail:

The spirits here aren't monsters or villains. According to the folklore and experiences I've gathered, they were once just...people. Community members. Friends. Children. Miners. Railmen. And just like any small town or neighborhood, some are grumpy. Happy. Sad. Silly.

Some are pranksters. Some just want to be heard.

You might hear a disembodied giggle or feel a playful tap on your shoulder. You might get called by name, or you might be teased a little by something with a sense of humor older than ours. And yes—every so often, you'll catch a growl, a sigh, or a whisper that sends chills up your spine.

The spirits along the trail have personalities. Some are kind. Some are curious. Some are just trying to get your attention. Most of the time, we don't even realize they're interacting with us until we watch the footage later— and then, it's like piecing together a message left in the static.

That's me on the right—usually, I'm the one behind the camera, so catching a photo of me is a rare thing!

So, if you're thinking about joining me, keep your eyes open, your ears sharp, and your expectations wide.

The ghosts don't always come when called—but when they do, they show up in unforgettable ways.

And with that... here are a couple of my favorite spots to haunt—

I mean hunt—and a few times (among many), we had an absolute blast with whoever (or whatever) decided to show up.

A Paranormal Investigation: Moonville Tunnel

Casey (center), Carson (left) and Caitlin (right) Knarr explore Moonville Tunnel—

Sparking student interest in science and technology can be a challenge—but teacher Casey Knarr goes above and beyond, introducing tech in unexpected and adventurous ways that capture students' imaginations. He even dives in himself, personally testing out paranormal research tools—then brings those experiences back to the classroom, where students are encouraged to analyze the data, debunk the findings, or draw their own conclusions based on the evidence.

And he's not just presenting it—he's living it.

One night, while I was out hiking with a group, I happened upon Casey, joined by a couple members of his family, Carson and Caitlin.

What started as a chance encounter turned into a night full of oddities—and just enough paranormal sass to keep things interesting.

Carson Meets a Ghost

It started at Moonville Tunnel, an old haunted stretch known for a few spirited pranksters. Carson, brave and curious, ventured into the tunnel solo, headlamp lit and voice steady as he asked questions aloud.

Carson (left) steps into the tunnel, unaware that within moments, something unseen will reach across the veil—and his view of the spirit world will never be the same.

That's when it happened—a heavy shove to his back with no one behind him.

At the exact moment, my video recorder outside picked up the eerie sound of children's giggles—faint, hushed, unmistakably ghostly.

Did I mention that Moonville has a few mischievous residents?

The Spirits Don't Like Our Knock-knock Jokes

That was also the night I broke out one of my spirit box favorites: the knock-knock joke. But as usual, the ghosts weren't having it.

"Knock-knock," I called.

A voice interrupted me with dry disdain: "Jannette, already heard that one."

I tried to press on: "Now, you gotta say, 'Who's there?'"

The spirit grumbled: "It's Mark. And you're sittin' in the dark."

I replied, "Olive. Now you say, 'Olive who?'"

Silence.

"Olive, you!" I proclaimed.

The spirit shot back, "Hello. And that's enough."

Me: "Do you think that's funny?"

Spirit: "No. Stupid."

Then another voice, saucy and bold, chimed in: "Classic brainstorm head."

(For the record, "brainstorm" was 1800s slang for "crazy." Noted.)

Casey wasn't fazed. He jumped in with his own knock-knock attempt.

"Knock-knock," he said.

Spirit: "I ain't gonna sit on *that* couch."

(A possible jab at psychologists... or just a vintage insult. Either way, bold move.)

Casey, still game: "Say, 'Who's there?'"

Spirit: "No."

Another chimed in: "No one."

Then a third, clearly unimpressed, announced: "They're strange."

Carson, chuckling, asked, "What's it like where you're at?"

And the spirit replied, softly but clearly: "Carson, this is like heaven here."

Caitlin Brings a Ghost to Her Knees

Later that evening, Caitlin sang an old-fashioned tune, a cappella. As her voice echoed with the haunting melody through the tunnel, a ghostly woman responded—not with words, but with a heartfelt, melancholic sigh, followed by a trembling whisper: "That's beautiful."

But the most bone-chilling moment may have come when the ghost train came through. Not literally, of course—but loud enough, deep enough, that the sound of grinding wheels was captured on video, unmistakable.

The Psych out

Earlier, Casey had asked the spirits, "When will the train come through?" and the spirit box responded: "Nine thirty-six."

And at 9:36—right on cue—it did.

Static crackled on the radio like a dispatcher's voice.

EMF detectors lit up in sync.

A sudden, icy gust swept through the tunnel, and everyone felt it.

Later, as Casey, Carson, and a fellow investigator named Shelby ran controlled tests to determine if cell phones were affecting the readings, they found that the EMF spikes were inconsistent with interference.

It was erratic.

Teasing.

Responsive.

Like someone—or something—was playing with them.

Finally, Shelby asked in a shaky voice, "Are you messing with us?"

The answer came back clear as day: "Psych out!"

It was a term straight from the 1960s, tossed back at us by something that clearly enjoyed the game.

And so did we.

A Paranormal Investigation: King/Mineral Tunnel

King Tunnel—also known as Mineral Tunnel—is one of the two shadowy corridors along the Moonville Rail Trail. Nestled between King's Station and Mineral, it yawns open in the hills like a mouth waiting to speak. Even before you see it, most people catch its scent first—the sharp, smoky tang of creosote clinging to the old wooden beams. And yes... it's haunted.

We know at least one young man lost his life inside its dark spine, and old stories claim he never truly left. But he's far from the only one. This stretch of track has witnessed more than its share of sorrow: brakemen crushed after sudden stops, a passenger who leapt too soon and broke his neck in the shallow creek, and rail workers who misjudged a step between cars and vanished beneath the wheels.

Then there's the girl. Some say the childlike giggles and faint chatter heard echoing from inside the tunnel belong to a little girl from Mineral—a schoolchild who drowned in the creek on her way home long ago.

One summer night, during a public hike and investigation at King Tunnel, we got more than we bargained for.

Rob and Terri Doyle, longtime members of the research team, have joined the hikes so regularly that when they miss one, even the ghosts notice—and ask where they are!

The forecast claimed a mere 10% chance of rain, but nature had other plans. As we reached the tunnel, thick black clouds rose fast, blotting out the moon. Thunder growled low across the hills, and lightning forked down the trail behind us like a warning. We ran. By the time the sky split open, we were taking shelter inside the gaping maw of King Tunnel, where rain came down in buckets and thunder cracked like musket fire overhead.

Using dowsing rods to spark ghostly conversation in King Tunnel.

The storm raged, and the air was charged with something more than electricity—it was like the tunnel had been waiting. During the investigation, we had the usual flickering lights and quiet whispers.

It whined, "He's not playing with me."

But the moment that stuck with all of us came when an uncle and his young nephew—drenched but determined—walked through the tunnel together. As they moved through the darkness, my video camera picked up a faint child's voice, almost sweet but whining, right next to the boy: "He's not playing with me."

Followed by soft, playful giggles.

There were no other children nearby. None laughing. None speaking. Just the storm outside... and something else within. That's King Tunnel.

It doesn't roar or scream. It waits—quiet and heavy—until you step just far enough inside to hear the whispers.

For Those Who Ask About Bigfoot at Moonville

There isn't a single night hike at Moonville where someone doesn't eventually ask:

"So... have you ever seen Bigfoot out here?"

It always comes from someone near the back of the group, the same one who's been nervously laughing since dusk and practically tripped over the first shadow we passed.

Sometimes, I'm not sure if they're asking because they genuinely want to know—or because they're trying to figure out just how far down the trail I've gone. But I've written about cryptids. I've talked to people who've seen things they can't explain. And I believe there are things out there—things we don't fully understand yet. So, I take the question seriously. Every time. Besides, I'd rather be out in the woods with the curious and the adventurous than stuck in an armchair with the skeptics, rolling their eyes and missing all the fun.

I always smile. And I say, "Well... let me tell you a story."

The Man on My Porch

Now, I live not far from Moonville. It's quiet. Remote. I don't get many visitors, and I'm fine with that. So when I stepped outside one morning and found a neighbor standing three feet from my porch, arms crossed and scowling like I owed him rent on the sunlight, I nearly backed right back inside and locked the door.

This was no friendly neighbor.

This was the kind who doesn't wave.

The kind of neighbor who'd been here so long, he probably considered anyone who moved in after the rotary phone an outsider. Which, unfortunately, included me.

The last time I saw him was ten years earlier when he marched up my driveway to inform me—very seriously—that people working for the local parks were dropping rattlesnakes into the forest. By parachute.

From airplanes.

Because the snake numbers were down.

And since I knew "park people," it was apparently my civic duty to put a stop to it.

When I laughed, he didn't. He stomped away and took off down the road in a cloud of gravel, and I figured I wouldn't see him again for another ten years—if ever. I planned to avoid him like the plague…which, admittedly, got a little inconvenient. People already think I'm odd thanks to my ghostly leanings, and in a town this small, ducking behind parked cars and slipping behind trees didn't exactly help my reputation.

Not the Dogs. Not the Skunks. Not the Snakes.

But there he was again, on my porch steps with arms crossed a decade later.

"Something's getting into my garbage," he said, voice flat.

Of course, I assumed he was here to blame my dogs. Granted, mine are fat, lazy, and built more for couch naps than rural crime—but I've seen them go feral over an old cheeseburger.

Still, they're fenced in. And not the kind of motivated to hike five miles just to score a banana peel.

I told him so. He sighed—like he'd just had to explain to a toddler that clouds aren't made of cotton candy.

"It's not a dog," he said.

"Skunk? Raccoon?"

"Nope."

"Coyote?"

"Nope."

"Bobcat?"

He stared at me.

"Something bigger."

"Bear?"

"No."

At this point, I was starting to think he came back after ten years just to make me say it.

He knew what he wanted me to ask.

I knew he knew.

And he knew I knew he knew.

The silence stretched so long that I started counting the cracks in the porch boards just to prove time was still moving.

Finally, I cracked like a three-year-old denied a cookie. "You're telling me... it might be Bigfoot?"

He didn't blink.

"I don't believe in that Bigfoot crap," he said. "But yeah."

Then he threatened me—gently.

"If you tell anyone about this before either of us is dead, one of us is gonna be sorry. And it ain't me."

And then he left.

No jig. No laughter. No parachuting snakes. Just the same dusty truck... and a story that bit harder the longer I sat with it.

My Own Eyes on the Trail

Of course, I never told him I'd had my own moment— because, true to form, he left in a hurry.

But that memory has stayed with me: quiet, unexplainable, and lodged in the back of my brain like a burr in a sock.

One night, near Bear Hollow along the Moonville Rail Trail, I spotted a pair of red eyes staring at me from just off the path. Naturally, I followed them—like a genius. Or, more accurately, like a cat with no survival instincts and a deep personal grudge against common sense. I knelt to get a better look, and that's when I realized the eyes were level with mine.

But they were on the other side of a cliff.

Whatever it was had to be ten feet tall—

Too high for a man. Too tall for a black bear.

Too steady for a deer.

Too real to laugh off.

And yet… I kept looking.

Because curiosity may not kill people the way it does cats, but it definitely makes us do some questionable trail choices after dark.

But My Neighbor Unlocked the Door

But once that door opened, the stories came pouring in—neighbors, hikers, strangers at the gas station.

Everyone had one.

And somehow, they all seemed to know I'd kept quiet about the old man, and I hadn't laughed at him—so I probably wouldn't rat them out either for their own "crazy Bigfoot stories."

Or maybe they just figured I had a few of my own, quietly tucked away. And they'd be right.

Because I still remember those red eyes at Bear Hollow—staring level with me from across a cliff, too high off the ground to belong to anything I should've been seeing out there.

I never did find out what it was.

But I didn't go looking for it, either.

Some stories don't need an ending to be true.

The Man Who Should've Held It

One of my favorites came from a woman in town whose cousin had a run-in just outside Moonville.

It's a local tradition—go out there late at night, try to find a ghost, then scream and flee in a cloud of gravel when something rustles in the brush.

That's just what you do.

This man was driving the road with his girlfriend, looking for a scare. What he found was... different.

Nature called, and he pulled over to relieve himself, stepping behind the car near the taillights while the headlights stayed on, casting long beams down the gravel road.

And then he saw it.

Across the hood of the car, in the edge of the light— something moved.

He straightened up. Squinted. Head tilted.

A shape came into view.

It stood upright.

Tall.

Too tall.

Hair all over.

Two eyes like glowing coals, staring right back at him.

He said it was 8 to 10 feet tall, hulking, breathing heavily, and not human.

Not a bear.

Not a joke.

Just standing there.

Watching.

Waiting.

He zipped up faster than any man has in recorded history and sprinted for the driver's seat. Slammed the door. Locked it. Gasped.

"Did you see that?" he asked his girlfriend, voice shaking.

She turned slowly. Face pale. Eyes wide.

"I did."

They left the road in a screaming blur of headlights and gravel.

So... Is There a Bigfoot at Moonville?

I'll let you decide.

But next time you come out here and hear something big and hairy stomping through the brush or catch red eyes glowing just beyond the treeline—don't say I didn't warn you.

It's probably not a dog.

And it's definitely not a parachuting rattlesnake.

Jannette Quackenbush

Citations

- Much of the core information about the towns and its peoples along with the folklore was collected from Bill Price in his interviews in the late 1950s when he was an Ohio State Park Naturalist. Part of his job was to research and collect everything he could of the town and its past. Without this research, we would know very little about the communities around Lake Hope State Park. Others, I have collected from neighbors, friends, and people who pass me in town at the grocery, the gas station, and sitting in the bleachers while my kids played high school sports.

Other notables:

- Quackenbush, Jannette. (n.d.). Moonville. Its Past. Its Ghosts. Its Legends. (Ghost Stories and Haunted Tales) (978-194008728 Columbus: 21 Crows Dusk to Dawn Publishing.
- Quackenbush, J. (2013). Haunted Hocking a Ghost Hunter's Guide to the Hocking hills ... and beyond: Ohio ghost hunter guide. 21 Crows Dusk to Dawn Publishing.
- Philadelphia Inquirer) October 14, 1889: Spooks and Spirits
- Athens Sunday Messenger November 10, 1963 newspaper Ohio University Archives, Mahn Center for Archives & Special Collections, Ohio University Libraries.
- Athens Sunday Messenger November 10, 1963, Believe in the Supernatural?
- Athens Sunday Messenger March 11, 1923
- Republican Enquirer. (McArthur, Ohio) March 29, 1920. Vinton County. 114 Years Ago in Vinton County History, By Our Route 2 Correspondent.
- Grabb, John R. The Marietta & Cincinnati Railroad and its successor, the Baltimore & Ohio: a study of this once great route across Ohio, 1851-1988.
- A collection and several interviews by Rich Dahn for a report in college.

- Year: 1920; Census Place: Chillicothe Ward 2, Ross, Ohio; Roll: T625_1431; Page: 15A; Enumeration District: 136
- Athens Sunday Messenger August 27, 1972 Price Bill. Strange Names. A Barrel. A Bog.
- Kathy Simcox, Historian. Interview with Clyde Pinney conducted by Kathy Simcox on February 23, 2003
- My own conversations with locals I bump elbows with at the grocery store, school sports, work, haunted night hikes at Moonville, and hiking around. The roots are deep in Vinton and Athens County and much of the folklore has been passed down and generously shared with me.
- Hope iron furnace schoolhouse and historical context. oldeforester.com/Hopeschs.htm
- Raw Head and Bloody Bones Origin: Scotch-Irish settlers Sources: WPA folklore projects (1930s), early Boone County oral Tradition
- Image of Red Landrum Wreck: Wreck Area (taken from the east) along one of the bleakest sections of the B & O between Hope Furnace Station and Moonville. Picture was taken 6 days after the wreck and crews had cleared much of the debris. You can still see rocks today from the fall. Image courtesy of the Estate of John R. Grabb. His book: The Marietta & Cincinnati railroad and its successor, the Baltimore & Ohio: a study of this once great route across Ohio, 1851-1988 hosts many images of trains in the region.